Starting with Serge

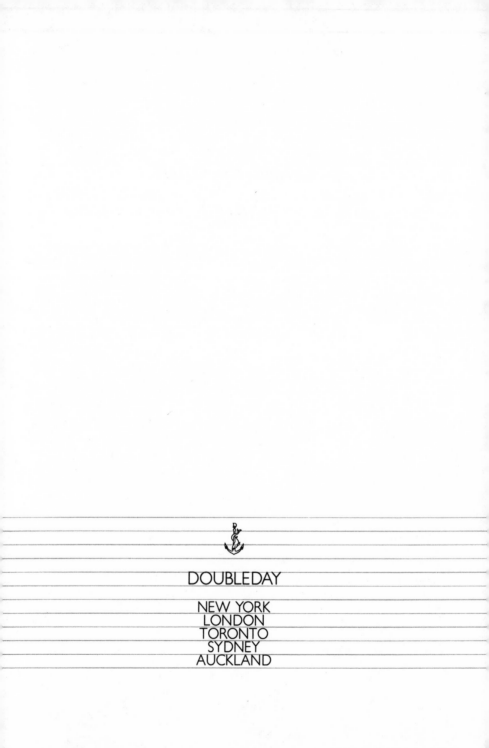

DOUBLEDAY

NEW YORK
LONDON
TORONTO
SYDNEY
AUCKLAND

Starting with Serge

LAURIE STONE

PUBLISHED BY DOUBLEDAY

a division of Bantam Doubleday Dell Publishing Group, Inc.
666 Fifth Avenue, New York, New York 10103

DOUBLEDAY and the portrayal of an anchor
with a dolphin are trademarks of Doubleday,
a division of Bantam Doubleday Dell Publishing
Group, Inc.

Library of Congress Cataloging-in-Publication Data
Stone, Laurie.
    Starting with Serge / by Laurie Stone. – 1st ed.
        p.   cm.
    ISBN 0-385-26308-2
    I. Title.
  PS3569.T64137S7   1990
813'.54–dc20   89-35387
                                                  CIP

All Rights Reserved
Printed in the United States of America
February 1990
FIRST EDITION
BG

For Murray Stone

To the Kittredge Fund and MacDowell Colony,
thanks for the money and time.

To M. Mark and Robert Myrstad,
thanks for early encouragement.

To Lucy Herring, Nan A. Talese, and Amanda Urban,
thanks for the perfect understanding.

To Janet Fisher, Margo Jefferson, Elizabeth Kendall,
and Gardner Leaver,
the deepest gratitude for making this book possible.

Starting with Serge

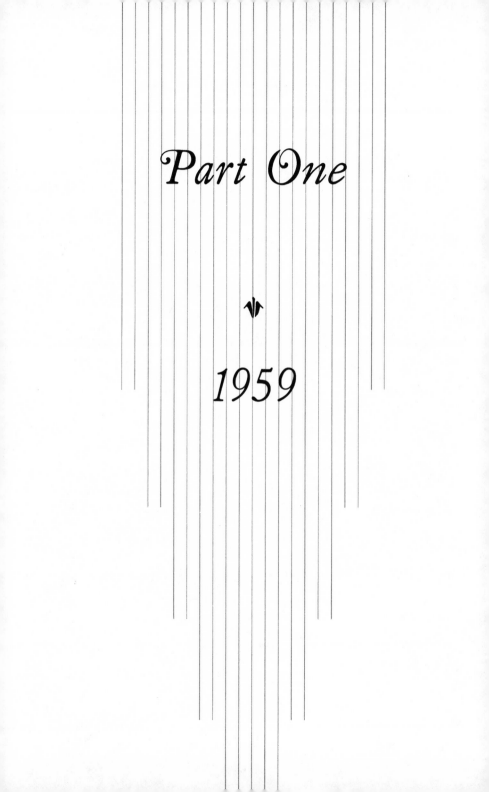

Part One

1959

Chapter 1

I DISCOVERED SERGE by listening at my parents' door. They kept saying, "shush," and shush sounded like Serge, so at first I was confused about his name, although I caught the phrase, "the best money can buy." Another day, when I barged into the living room, my parents shut up, whispering, *die Kleine*, but not before I heard my father say, "brilliant psychiatrist." Serge, I gathered, was the best psychiatrist money could buy. From the beginning he was Serge, never Dr. Lodst.

We got Serge because of Madelyn, my sister, even though she'd always seemed the most normal. She'd danced on "American Bandstand," wearing a tight sweater and straight skirt. The camera had gone in for a close-up, and she'd smiled like a cat. I expected to be her when I grew up, but she didn't leave many clues.

When she called that Saturday night, I saw the color drain from my father's face. He shooed me from the living room. When he came out, he grabbed my mother by the wrist and pulled her into their bedroom. Half an hour later they exited, my mother carrying an overnight case.

"We're getting Madelyn," my father said.

"Did she flunk?"

"How could you think your sister would flunk?" my mother shot.

It was easy. Madelyn hated studying. But I figured the trouble was worse. I was the youngest and the last to know everything, or so I thought. Not knowing made me dream up disasters.

"She's tired." My father kissed the top of my head and walked to the door. "You know how to take care of yourself."

Lines like that made me want to burn down the house.

The next day, at six, I heard the Oldsmobile crunching on the gravel, and I peered out the window. My sister got out of the car, looking confused. Her coat wasn't buttoned right. There were brownish circles under her eyes, and her hair hung in greasy strands. She'd put on weight, maybe fifteen pounds, enough to make her look puffy and soft. This couldn't be Madelyn, the girl kids always imitated. At camp, we even sang the way she did: flat.

I hugged her. Her face was unreadable, but that wasn't unusual. Madelyn was the only one who didn't register every emotion, like ticker tape. She glanced at her red suede shoes. They were muddy, even though it was dry out. She'd worn them on purpose.

Any other day, my mother would have screamed, "Get those shoes off the rug." But now she was counting my sister's luggage, a cigarette hanging off her bottom lip. "What about the gray? You left it, right?"

"It's over there, Thee." My father pointed to the corner of the den. "We got everything."

She kept counting. I helped my father set the table and line up cartons of Chinese food. We didn't put it in bowls, and we didn't talk.

At dinner, Madelyn, who'd always been indifferent to food, gulped down egg rolls and lobster, barely chewing. After a while, she turned green and began to gag, but she made no move to get up. I laughed. My parents stared, then my mother put her hand over Madelyn's mouth and led her to the bathroom. My father walked behind, murmuring, "That's okay, baby. Let it out."

It was just like my sister to explain herself in the form of a vomit. If I'd been able to read it–like tea leaves or entrails–I would have followed them. Instead I went to the den, taking my usual seat beside the room divider, one of Stuart the decorator's more dramatic selections. It was made of semitransparent plastic, into which were embedded pieces of wheat and whole, real butterflies. I stared at the butterflies, feeling as pressed as they were by all the secrets I didn't know.

In my parents' idea of progress, the past did not live inside you, expanding and contracting like the pleats on an accordion; it kept getting detached, like defunct railway cars from a speeding train. I had only the sketchiest knowledge of what had come before me—like if there was madness in our family. I knew my parents had grown up on the Lower East Side, but I had few pictures of this life. When I'd ask my parents about their childhoods, they'd say, "We were poor. Sometimes we were very poor. What's to remember?"

The only thing my father liked recalling was going on the road. He'd crane his neck forward, and his voice would grow husky. He'd make his life sound like a lucky gamble, an unlikely deal he'd somehow closed. And he was always a man in his descriptions. Even Herschel the boy wore a pin-striped suit and a broad-brimmed hat.

I can't remember a time when I didn't know this story: My father quit school at fourteen and got a job as a traveling salesman. He toured New England, selling lingerie and ladies' dresses. The first year, he hired a driver for his car. At fifteen, he lied about his age and finagled a license. Then he worked his way up, covering larger and larger territories, finally saving enough to make his own line. Now he manufactured coats for girls, and the business kept expanding. He loved adorning females. He'd follow pretty women down the street, pad and pen in hand, and copy the pleats in their skirts, the collars on their blouses.

With my mother, the past glinted from a strange photograph, not the kind you'd expect to see in a family album. She was ten or eleven, standing on a city street wearing a ragged white dress, the hem of which hung unevenly around her white-

stockinged legs. She was beautiful. Her cheekbones jutted promi-
nently and her eyes were slanted. But she looked blitzed, frozen
with dread, as if something threatening lay just outside the frame
of the picture. She'd stare at it, grinning weirdly. "It must have
been awful," she'd say.

"How awful?" I'd ask.

She'd turn the page as if slamming a door. "You want me to
dig up pain to satisfy your curiosity? Get another guinea pig."

Each of my parents had a living parent, in whom I might
have discerned something of their pasts, but the pieces didn't fit.
My optimistic father had had, I thought, a bad deal, which
explained nothing, except perhaps his eagerness to hit the road.
My grandfather had been a pants presser, and I knew him as a
slow, wrinkled old man who showed little emotion. When we
visited him in the Bronx, I'd watch my father hold the old man's
thin shoulders and brush his lips across a tanned, leathery cheek.
In Yiddish, my father would ask about my grandfather's health,
meals, and exercise regime, and then my grandfather would ask
the same questions of his son, puffing a cigar, staring into space.
I never saw him tease my father or ruffle his hair. Was he proud
of his son? My father, who supported my grandfather, acted
more like the parent.

My mother, on the other hand, appeared to have been
loved. My grandmother would hear us on the stairs of her
Brooklyn apartment, her door would open, and cooking smells
would leap into the hall before she could reach us herself and
squash us against her large bosom. Strands of gray hair would fall
across her eyes. Grease stains spotted her housedress. She'd
move, dervishlike, between the oven, where the noodle kugel
was baking, to the stove, where barley and mushroom soup was
simmering, thick as tar, to the table, covered with pirogen,
chicken, and chopped liver. With cheeks red from cooking and
eyes dancing, she'd pop potato pancakes into bubbling fat, all
the time talking in rapid-fire Yiddish, explaining which actors
were Jewish and which were not, keeping her eyes glued to my

mother. She'd ask the ceiling to explain her modern daughter, as my mother laughed at her superstitious spitting and hysterical reactions to sneezes. They'd hold each other, rocking and crooning, "Mama, Mama."

So there they were: my father the fortunate traveler and my mother the displaced waif. And I couldn't tell how much of each depiction was true and how much fabrication.

Madelyn finished gagging, and the toilet flushed. My father came into the den, sat beside me, and put his arm around my shoulder. My head slipped into his armpit. "What's wrong with Madelyn?"

"She's upset. She'll be all right." He waved his hand. "What did you do today, love?"

"Saw Amy, flipped Elvis cards, won a stack off Kathy Sachs." I was better at lying than my father; my voice didn't crack and I could meet his eyes. In fact, I'd gone to the Archer Street canal and tried to get the tough boys to notice me. One had, lifting a horseshoe crab by its stinger, twirling it over his head like a lasso, and hurling it in my direction. I'd fled, satisfied, my shoes sinking in the muddy sand.

My father picked up the remote control and flicked on the TV. The device was his latest gadget. My father liked anything modern.

"Put on Ed Sullivan," my mother said, coming in. To me: "Get on the other couch."

Jackie Mason appeared on screen. "If you lived here a year, already you were a Yankee."

"I love him," my mother said. "He's such a Jew." She went to the "S" volume of the Encyclopaedia Britannica, reached behind it, and pulled out a jumbo Hershey bar. She broke off a piece and gave it to my father. I held out my hand, and she scrunched up her face in disbelief. "You cry about being fat, then want chocolate?"

"Yeah."

"I'm the one who has to shop with you and see your frustration."

I twirled a clump of hair, making it stiff.

"Don't do that, darling." She drew the hair from my hands. "Oy, that Madelyn. I have to watch her like a hawk." She smoothed my hair, tucking it behind an ear. "Not like you."

I flicked the hair out. My mother sighed. Jackie Mason said, "You were either poor, or very poor," and as my parents said, "You see?" I went to the kitchen and got an apple and an orange. No one argued with me about fruit. When I came back, my father's arm was around my mother, and their heads were touching. My father kissed her cheek. "Where did you get such a good-looking mother?"

She was beautiful, a blond with a sleek figure and green eyes. My father was attractive too, with a body muscled from handball and dark hair waving off his forehead. His delicate brows and long-lidded brown eyes seemed especially emotional in his man's face–like dog eyes.

My parents said Madelyn and I were good-looking too, and anyone seeing us would take us for their children; we had our father's eyes and mother's diamond-shaped face. But my parents were handsomer than either of their children. They needed to be.

We watched TV, while Madelyn stayed in her room–our room–the one we'd shared but which had since become mine, and now who knew? We watched TV every Sunday night, but it was a Sunday like no other. College meant progress, and now Madelyn had gone seriously off course.

At eleven, I dragged myself to bed, and when I spotted Madelyn's suitcases in front of the closet, I wanted to kick them in and scatter the contents. Then I saw my sister, looking like an outsized Alice in the White Rabbit's shrinking parlor. "I love you," I said, dropping my clothes on the floor.

"I know, doll." Her voice was slow.

I slipped on my nightgown. "What's wrong? You don't look right."

"I don't *feel* right."

"What happened at college? Please tell." My stomach was hurting from not knowing.

"Nothing, doll. I just got tired." She yawned.

"Stop lying."

"Oh, Julie, stop *digging*. Go to sleep."

"Go to hell," I said, and pulled the covers over my head.

*

I thought we were headed upward, my father steering us. My grandparents had fled Poland and Russia, where people were poor and unhappy. My parents had fled the Lower East Side, progressing to Washington Heights.

The neighborhood they entered was divided into two parts. East of Broadway was noisy and jumping, with Woolworth's, the Automat, two movie theaters, and St. Nicholas Avenue, where grocers gave out free tastes; and children, chomping rolls and cheese, skipped behind their mothers. Vendors sold yams and chestnuts in greasy paper cones. From time to time, children were lifted over gutters to pee, and the air pulsed with foreign words. Italian kids munched sausages. Puerto Rican girls wore ruffly dresses. Cuban men, who, at all hours, twirled and licked leaves in the nearby cigar factory, watched over the neighborhood.

The west side of Broadway, where the German Jews lived, was another country. The air was still. Thick trees shaded the streets, and the buildings rose up grand and massive. It was dull, but the peaceful atmosphere, the grave-sounding German language, and the reserve of the residents—who waited in orderly lines at the bakery and strolled sedately in Fort Washington Park —radiated learning and control. This was class—a stratum, a state of mind—which my parents yearned to attain.

Our apartment was on the border, a fitting perch between streets smelling of the past and others redolent of our intended future. My memories of Washington Heights are mostly sunny, partly because we were hopeful then and partly because of my father's home movies, in which we always look yellow–burnished by sun or blazing indoor lights.

Teresa Brewer, with her unearthly child's voice–or Rosemary Clooney, or Tony Bennett–would sing on the radio, while my sister headed for school and my father set out for Eighth Avenue. Then I had my mother. She'd drink coffee and smoke cigarettes. I'd eat Cream of Wheat, then lick the bowl. I'd sit on her bed, whooshing my arms and legs across the satin coverlet, as she inched stockings over slim calves and thighs.

We'd walk to Wadsworth Avenue, past P.S. 132, where Madelyn was ensconced, past the toy store with its menagerie of stuffed animals. Every so often, my mother would squeeze my hand in pulse beats, or I'd do it to her. At the butcher's, I was given a salami end to munch. In the A&P, I rode the shopping cart, my eyes trained on my mother's face, as she struggled to remember what she'd come to buy. At the Automat, I'd wait on the balcony, watching her move down the line, thread her way through the tables and climb the stairs, where she'd vanish–making my heart pound–then reappear, swaying on her high heels.

At the schoolyard, my sister would be jumping rope, defying the snaky whip, her ponytail bobbing, her face concentrated on the rhythm. I admired the way she said "Hi," casual, nonchalant, and the way she played ringalievo, running wildly, the boys in pursuit. The word "ringalievo" sent chills up my spine. My mother and I would watch the blur of movement, hear the insect-buzz of sound, and it would seem Madelyn belonged to the schoolyard, but once outside the iron fence, she'd grab my mother's hand and I'd clasp hers, and we'd walk home in size order.

Madelyn would "watch me," meaning we could roam our

block but not cross streets. My sister would organize hide-and-seek games and set up hurdles with boxes left outside the A&P. The kids would shout to their mothers, "Drop me a dime," then shriek with pleasure as the coins, wrapped in newspaper, made their unpredictable journeys, sometimes landing on the hoods of cars. Then it was off to the candy store to buy miniature soda bottles made of wax and filled with intensely sweet liquid. Or else dots, costing two cents a sheet and lasting forever.

At five, I'd have a bath, then zoom to the living room to watch puppets on TV: Pinhead and Foodini; Kukla and Ollie; Howdy Doody and Mr. Bluster. In front of the TV—caged in a solemn mahogany box—sat a leather hassock, and behind that a couch. Brilliant dahlias swam across its slipcovers. I'd plop myself on the hassock and watch the puppets abuse each other, all the time waiting for Madelyn to sneak up and charge, as she inevitably would, and displace me like a croquet ball.

My sister and I would be eating dinner when my father's key rattled in the door. We'd race to meet him, hanging on his arms, pulling down his face for kisses. He'd kiss my mother, who'd be cutting grapefruits. As my bedtime approached, my sister would look superior, and I'd plead for time. That failing, I'd say, "Lay with me," to my father, and he'd take me to my room, stretch out beside me, and ask what story I wanted—a mere formality, because I always said "Cinderella." He'd recite it by heart, while I studied the patterns made by passing headlights. They'd come up small and bright, fan out quickly, then vanish, making way for another, again and again.

⚜

The move from Manhattan came when I was seven. Washington Heights was "too Spanish." The best place for kids was "the country." Luna Island–a ten-mile spit forty miles from the city–was targeted the year I entered third grade.

I'd discovered nature at camp: rolling down lawns, arms by my sides, caterpillars squishing underneath, dragonflies mating above. But on Luna Island I became a citizen of nature. My mother didn't worry about where I went, and my quickly won best friend, Amy Jack, taught me to walk the jetties and scour the shore. At first Madelyn missed her friends, but after a few months she became a cheerleader and said no more about Washington Heights. We thought she was happy. We always thought that.

My parents stopped seeing most of their relatives, including my mother's three brothers: Duddy, Yosel, and Jake–beefy guys who laughed a lot and were partners in a warehouse. My father had brothers too. Saul, the oldest, owned a hardware store in Bridgeport. Aaron, the youngest, sold hot dogs and pretzels at the Bronx zoo. (Later, he worked for my father. Eventually, he wound up behind the counter with Saul.) Saul looked like a Marx brother, except for his expression, which said, "I've been gypped." The uncle Aaron I remember was jittery and thin. He looked like Kafka. In all Jewish albums, there is always an uncle who looks like a Marx brother and another like Kafka.

My parents saw less of my grandparents too. The only relative still prized was Wolf, my father's third brother–Wolf, the fancy, exciting uncle, who sold antiques and was richer than my father.

Despite these changes, suburban life failed to engage my parents. My mother went to a PTA meeting. "It's not for me," she said upon returning. She joined a temple and ran the gift shop, selling crocheted yarmulkas and menorahs with turquoise chips in them. She didn't like that either. On Luna Island, where Jews were safe and powerful, it was harder for her to feel like an underdog, in other words, Jewish. Next, she volunteered at the hospital, where she made sodas and sandwiches at the luncheonette– "to kill time." Summers, she let her shoulders bake at the beach club and played mah-jongg, distractedly moving her pieces. She'd walk to the ocean and wade to her knees, never farther—she didn't know how to swim. When our house was remodeled, my father insisted that everything be new, and my mother went shopping with the decorator. She didn't exactly trust him, because she didn't trust anybody, but she gave herself up to his taste because, despite what she said to the contrary, she didn't have faith in her own taste at all. As the new things arrived, she dubbed them, and thereafter referred to them, as "Stuart's lamp," "Stuart's chair," "Stuart's couch."

My father joined the Kiwanis Club. "It's not for me," he said. A gleaming set of golf clubs sat unused in his closet. The barbecue he bought was never lit. We mostly ate out, and my parents didn't entertain. Restless on weekends, my father would drive to the track alone, unable to persuade my mother to go along. The only thing he liked was the beach, diving through the waves, shaking water from his hair.

Friday nights, my mother would join my father in the city, and they'd go to nightclubs, shows. Some Sundays, they'd prowl the Lower East Side and return with gefilte fish, hard salami, kasha varnishkes, and pirogen. I'd ask how the old neighborhood was, and they'd say, "Horrible. Horrible then and horrible now." But they kept going back.

They stuck out the suburbs "for the kids." By the time my sister went to college, I was bored too. So here we were, having made all the right moves, yet finding ourselves stalled. And now that Madelyn was home, we had to admit it.

The first week my sister was back, she acted crazy on and off, and my parents let her do what she wanted. I went along too. By midweek, she was eager to get out of the house. "Let's drive," she'd say, but she couldn't leave Luna Island. She'd cruise, come to a bridge, and head in another direction.

Wednesday afternoon, we toured Port Olive, where the fishermen lived, then Breaker Shore, a warren of narrow streets and tiny bungalows. We explored the oldest section, Coral Grove, with its sturdy brick houses, then Star Beach, the newest development of colonials and sod lawns. We drove by the ancient resort hotels which, like their tenants, sat on the boardwalk and stared out to sea. We surveyed our own neighborhood, the canals, where six little bay inlets notched the land. Finally we parked at the boardwalk.

The ocean smelled strong, and gulls were crying overhead. The wind was up, and Madelyn pulled a scarf from her pocket and tied it under her chin. We leaned against the railing, looking at the green-gray waves. She flashed a crooked smile. "Ma said you had a date. How come you didn't tell?"

"Stop smirking."

"I'm not."

"You always do. Besides, it was nothing, a movie with Peter Katz. I don't even like him." Peter came up to my chin but was the best I could do.

"Why'd you go?" She leaned back authoritatively.

"He asked."

"Next time say no."

"Yeah?"

"Um hmm." She stuck her chin in the air. "Remember Miller?" She walked.

"Of course." Miller was her first boyfriend. I knew their relationship chapter and verse.

"Remember when he made me eat pizza?"

"Yeah."

"I thought I'd drop dead."

"Mom said it was poison and you believed her."

"I didn't."

"You did."

"Didn't you?"

"Are you kidding?"

She walked faster. "Remember Miller's Chevy?"

"I was *there*."

"Oh yeah. That car looked like a wreck, but it could peel out. Miller must have done something to it. He was good with his hands." She gave me the look that promised dangerous secrets: a half smile, one eyebrow up, her chin at an angle. I'd always gone for it. But in light of the things she wasn't saying, I resisted the temptation.

She went on, "Let's play ski ball—no, let's go to the shooting gallery." Her voice was high, urgent. She grabbed my hand. I let her lead and stood to the side while she shot at targets. Whatever was wrong with her, it hadn't affected her aim. She brought down two bears and a buffalo and won a plastic doll with red feathers covering its breasts and bottom. The man running the concession held it out, and Madelyn snatched it, stuffing it in her pocket as if she were stealing.

We stood by the railing again, Madelyn leaning on her elbows, taking deep breaths.

"Sisters?" an old woman asked. She was sitting on a bench. Next to her was another old woman and an old man. The first woman was thin and tan, and her crinkled features rose with hope.

Madelyn played deaf.

"Yes," I blurted.

"You love each other," the second woman said.

I couldn't tell if she was asking a question or giving an order. She was tanned, too, but small and round.

"Yeah, sure."

Madelyn turned away, but I could see the shadow of a smile on her face. The old women were casting glances at each other too. They seemed intimate, like they'd been together a long time.

"Are *you* sisters?" I ventured.

"Ach," the thin woman barked. "We meet on this bench. We have nobody, and we are old, so maybe we look alike to you."

"You don't." They did.

"There are worse things than being alone," the old man said, lifting an eyebrow and smiling ruefully. "But not many."

"Sweet girls," the plump woman offered, gazing at the sky and opening her palms.

"Children saved from the war," the man added, looking from me to Madelyn, trying to find something in us about the war and the Nazis, but there was nothing there. My parents didn't say any more about the war than about their own pasts.

"What war?" Madelyn said, looking alarmed.

The thin woman's jaw dropped, and her eyes narrowed. The plump woman and the man looked outraged.

"Hitler," the thin woman said, her voice frozen.

"Oh, Hitler." Madelyn said, sounding relieved.

The trio darkened, clucking their tongues and asking the clouds for an explanation for such wicked, ignorant children. Madelyn's eyes got just as black. "I wasn't saved from any war and neither was *she.*"

She grabbed my arm. I laughed.

She moved fast. "Ma thinks I know nothing. Miller wanted to fuck me."

"Did you?"

"Nuh uh."

"How come?"

She shrugged. She was drifting again. There was something I wanted to tell her, and I didn't want to let her go.

"Listen," I said momentously. "Rudy Corso said sperm comes out the same hole as pee." She made a face. "*Stop smirking,*" I shouted.

"I'm not."

"You are."

"Rudy Corso's horrible."

"He's not." He was fourteen and conceited, but I loved him.

When he told me about sperm, my breath felt like it was being sucked out with a vacuum cleaner. "*Sperm* sounds horrible."

"Not if you're in love."

"How do you know?" I saw her on a bed, naked. Maybe sperm had made her crazy.

She stopped. "I'm eighteen, I'm supposed to." She stretched her arms and twirled. "Miller's gonna be a doctor. I could probably get him back. Should I?" She shoved my shoulder.

She'd dumped Miller in her junior year, even though he adored her. After Miller, there was Ray, and after him Manny. I didn't know what she should do. I shrugged.

She rubbed her hands together. "Let's have some *real* fun." I thought she was going to suggest a joyride to Port Olive, flooring it all the way. Instead, in a little-girl voice she said, "Let's go on the Tilt-a-Whirl." She ran to the ride, not looking to see if I was behind, not needing to.

We climbed into a car. The attendant clicked the safety bar in place, and as the gears began to grind and the speed increased, Madelyn shouted, "lean." I pressed against her, feeling the length of her, and she was mine, as she'd always been.

I was five the summer I first went to camp. My parents became specks, like the stars which shot across the Catskill sky, then fizzled to nothing. I learned to swim in the deep water, cutting through black liquid, staying afloat. Before meals, I'd spot my sister at the flagpole and fling myself at her, wrapping my arms around her waist, braiding my legs through hers. No rule or regulation could stop me.

Faster and faster the Tilt-a-Whirl turned. In the speed, I forgot my sister's troubles. I forgot everything but the next breathless breath. We spun so wildly, I thought our heads would fly off, and just at that instant Madelyn's scarf escaped in the wind and I thought her head actually had come off. It was just for a moment, until her hair billowed out, but it seemed like I'd lost her while I remained. My mouth tasted of dirt.

When the ride stopped, I blurted, as if in penance, "Amy doesn't like me anymore."

"What are you talking about? I hear you on the phone all the time."

"I call her."

"She talks, doesn't she?"

"It's not the same. We used to tell each other everything."

Once, she'd dared me to leap from the second-story window of a house under construction. I'd landed in a sandpile, amazed I'd done it. We'd said we'd marry when we grew up, unable to decide who would be the girl and who the boy.

"We were as close as this." I twisted two fingers. "She got her period and kept it a secret."

"So?"

"I felt awful."

It had happened a month ago, in the upstairs bathroom of Amy's house. It happened the day I discovered blood in my own underpants. "Come here," I screamed. She came to the door. "Look," I said. My adrenaline was pumping. I was faint with happiness and fear.

"Oh," she said, quiet.

"Isn't it exciting?"

"Yeah." She wouldn't meet my eyes.

"What's the *matter?*"

She stared at me. "I got mine already."

"When?"

"Six months ago."

"How come you didn't say anything?"

"My mother said not to." She sounded pained. "I was supposed to wait till you got yours. Oh, I don't know." She kept her distance. "Ma!" she hollered.

Ginger Jack came in, and Amy told her about me. They stood close. With their blue eyes and downy skin, they looked like sisters. Ginger approached, smiling. She was the mother who baked cookies and didn't yell. I thought she was going to kiss me,

but instead she slapped my face. "*Mazel tov*. You're a woman."
She fetched a Kotex pad and a belt. I was supposed to feel my life
was beginning, but it seemed that everything good was in the
past.

Madelyn put her arm around my shoulder. "Maybe she felt
shy."

"We used to do strip dances in front of each other."

She raised an eyebrow. "Maybe she wants to be friends
differently."

"She hates me."

"Oh, Julie, you're exaggerating. You always do. I came
home, so you want attention. Amy doesn't hate you. Give her
room. Give *me* room. Don't be jealous of me now."

I stared at her. She sounded sane. I watched the waves.
They were growing calmer as the tide went out. I didn't know if
I was exaggerating.

Madelyn ruffled my hair. "Things don't stay the same, but it
doesn't have to be bad." She drew me along. She looked worldly,
filled with experience I couldn't imagine and didn't want to. It
was nice to float beside her, being the younger one with problems an older sister could dismiss. But a moment later, she bolted
to a cotton candy vendor, and I knew something scary was
coming. I didn't know what it was, or maybe I did. Maybe it was
staying where we were, living in a house like ours and ricochet-
ing through the neighborhoods on an endless bumper-car ride.

Madelyn pulled off tufts of cotton candy with her fingers.
Then she ducked behind me, pointing and croaking, "There's
Nora Holtz." Nora was in the distance, barely recognizable. Nora
commuted to nursing school and had been one of Madelyn's best
friends.

"So?"

"Don't be a jerk." She thrust the cotton candy in my hands
and dug in her pockets, finding the Kewpie doll. "Where's my
scarf?"

"It blew off on the ride. Didn't you know?"

She shook her head, staring at the doll. It stuck first to one gluey hand, then the other. She tore at it violently, desperately, and the feathers flew off with shocking ease. It was nearly naked, and I saw it had no sexual parts, except for a crease meant to represent its ass. I grabbed it. "Throw it away," she said, but I couldn't.

"What'll I do?" she whined. "She'll *see* me." She gripped my wrists.

"You don't look so bad." The circles under her eyes had disappeared, and she'd lost weight.

"You don't know *what* I look like, and you don't care." She released me, snagging some hairs. "Run."

She bent her head and darted away. She jogged steadily, easily, while I loped behind, panting. After a mile, I reached her. She was leaning against the car, looking masterful and strong, as if she'd won a race. And the thought crossed my mind that she'd faked the confusion of the last few days, faked everything. It wasn't fair. At Christmas, she'd come home talking about a ski weekend, and I'd seen her streaking into the stratosphere. She was supposed to go away and stay there.

"Get in," she said, opening her door.

I did. The doll fell out of my pocket and rolled under the right front wheel. I left it, but when Madelyn backed out and I heard it crunch between the tire and the sand, I felt I'd aged past youth, with no hope of return.

⇟

Saturday, Madelyn saw Serge for the first time, although I didn't know it. I thought she was in the city to sell coats. Saturdays, my father sold retail.

"Let's go to the Oasis?" my mother said at breakfast. The Oasis was a mammoth shopping center, another place my mother went "to kill time." "We can schmooze around, then shop for food." She put a bagel on my plate and sipped coffee.

"Okay." I liked to be alone with her, even when she was jumpy and bored. Alone was the only way I liked her.

We packed into the Plymouth, and she said, "The Chinese laundry lost our bundle. I hope it winds up in China."

I laughed.

She lit a cigarette, turning on the radio. "Who's that?"

"The Shirelles."

She shook her head. "You know everything. You were maybe two when you memorized the *Hans Christian Andersen* album." She kissed my hand. "Pearl found these shoes on sale. There's no one like her. How could there be? Everybody's one of a kind. The shoes were too small, but she told the salesman, 'I have obedient toes.'" My mother snorted, waiting for me to laugh. She dragged on her cigarette. "Other people accept. They're better off." She tossed the stub out the window and looked at me. I pointed to the road. She said, "Amy's mother has a lovely garden."

"Uh ha."

"She gave you tulip bulbs?"

"You know she did."

"I forget whether it was gladiolas or tulips. What do I know from flowers?" She lit another cigarette. "The whipped cream wouldn't stop squirting."

"What whipped cream?"

"What do you mean 'What whipped cream'? Where do I go beside the hospital? Honestly. So I'm making a sundae for this guy. I shake the can and start squirting, and it won't stop. 'Pearl,' I scream. She's making a tuna fish sandwich, but she runs over and lines up glasses. I shoot in whipped cream, and she puts cherries on top and sells them as charlotte russes. My guy she gives it to for free. Ooh was he handsome . . . either a lawyer or an accountant. Personally, I can't stand either one. Pearl said he liked me but I'm too stupid to know. The things I get into. I should have my own TV show." She searched my eyes. I looked out the window. She put out her cigarette, and another song played on the radio. "Who's that?"

"The Coasters."

"I love them. 'Poison i–ve-ee-ee-eee!' Imagine, they made a song about that. Remember when you had it?"

"I had poison sumac."

"Yeah? Well, you swelled up like a balloon. 'Poison i–vee-ee-ee-eee!' Maddy danced to this on Dick Clark. Boy can she dance." She jabbed me with her elbow. "So can you. I didn't raise klutzes." We drove onto Main Bridge, and the lights began flashing. She turned off the engine while the bridge opened and a boat passed through. "Where do you think it's going?" she asked in an excited voice.

"The city?"

She shook her head, cocky. "Farther. Look at the flags. Look at the cabin." She drummed her nails on the steering wheel. "God I hate this town."

"There's the beach."

She leaned her head back and shut her eyes. "I don't care if I never see another wave."

We continued, past a parade of towns, with their sleepy main streets, lone movie theaters, and Chinese restaurants. Past shuttered houses, manicured lawns, azaleas, and lawn jockeys. Twenty minutes later, we arrived at the Oasis: fifteen miles of shoes copied from Capezio and dresses knocked off from Lanz. The atmosphere was festive, everyone full of expectation, the air smelling of hot dogs, pizza–the closest thing here to street life. My mother got into it, moving with confidence, grabbing my hand and squeezing it in pulse beats. It seemed my bones were soft, like fish bones.

We were heading for the junior department in Appleseed's department store, when a hat caught my mother's eye. She plunked the fox pouf on her head and pulled it down to her nose.

"Your mother." Her nostrils quivered. She looked beautiful. "I could have been a model."

"I know." My voice was flat.

"How could you?"

"You told me."

"I never did."

"A hundred times."

"You exaggerate."

I raised an eyebrow. She looked in the mirror. "You have no idea how gorgeous I was."

"I do."

"How could you?"

"From pictures."

"They don't do me justice." She took off the hat. "There was this buyer where I worked. Eight dollars a week to stand on my feet forty-eight hours. He gave me a card. 'My friend's a photographer,' he said. 'He'll pay to take your picture.' Can you imagine the life I would have led? The people I would have met?"

"Who?"

She screwed up her mouth. "You ask the oddest questions." We walked. "I was thrilled somebody should notice me. I wanted my mother to say *'Mazel tov.'* But she made a face and said, 'Are you crazy?' That's how she talked. She said the photographer was bad. I didn't believe her, but I listened."

"How come?"

"Because I was a rag and she was iron."

"Grandma doesn't seem like that."

She stopped. "She's old. She lost her fangs. You should have seen her then."

"Tell me."

Her head jerked back. "I don't remember." She scanned the displays and rushed us to a rack of "manufacturer's samples," her eyes gleaming at the extravagantly marked-down prices. She gathered several outfits and led me to a dressing room. "Have I got an eagle eye?"

"Yes, Mom." I slipped on a dress. The waist bunched up grotesquely. I lumbered and grunted like Quasimodo.

She shrieked, collapsing against the mirrors. "I'm gonna pee." She crossed her legs. Tears ran down her cheeks. "Stop. I mean it. Don't look at me. No, really don't, Julie." She clutched her stomach. "We're gonna get sick."

We kept it up. We had to turn our backs, but even then giggles kept erupting.

Sometimes, my mother could rise up clear. Once when I was little, we heard a creak, then a loud crash, as the sink fell off the wall in the bathroom. Water gushed, flooding the bedroom. "The rug, the drapes, the wallpaper," she shouted, but she was also laughing, seeing the futility of rescuing the things. She jumped on the bed, threw back her head, and grabbed me around the waist. She held me for only an instant, but the time fanned out so that it seemed we were marooned on an island and she'd become a little girl. Then she took my hand, and we sloshed through the water. I wanted to play in it, but she was an engine of purpose now, racing down six flights to the super.

I tried on the other dresses, but they didn't look good. Back at the racks, I picked out a black jumper with a matching bolero jacket. My mother's pleasure drained. I could hear it, a pop. "That's not right." She tugged at the material. "You wanna look thirty? Maybe you could wear it to a funeral."

"Whose?"

A saleswoman approached. "How's everything, girls?"

My mother stared. "We'll ask for help when we need it."

The saleswoman backed off.

My mother talked loud. "When you want them they hide in the stockroom, the rest of the time they're on top of you."

The saleswoman turned. I shrugged an apology. My mother caught it and looked at the ceiling. "She's nice to strangers, to strangers she's nice. But they don't know what she is."

"Stop," I pleaded. "You're acting nuts."

She looked blitzed, like in the photograph. "You're dead." She sped away.

"Come on, don't fight about a *saleswoman*. We were having fun."

"Fun with you? You drain my blood. Traitor!"

We raced past scarves and jewelry. We parted crowds. "I'm sorry."

"You're *always* sorry."

I plucked at her arm. "Really." I grabbed her hand, but she pulled it away. I grabbed it again, squeezing it in pulse beats. She stopped. Walking back, she looked like a lost child, uncertain she wanted to find her family. At the dress racks, I said, "Show me which one you like." I pulled out a yellow outfit with orange stripes. "How's this?"

"It's from hunger. You picked it on purpose. Oh, you, you." She searched the racks, but her hopefulness was gone. She guided me to a dressing room, and I tried on what she picked. She stood back, a fist under her chin. "Nuh uh." I slipped on another, and she clapped her hands. "Oh my God. It's gorgeous, and *so slimming.*" She slunk to her knees and hunted for pins, sticking three between her teeth, hiking up the hem.

The dress made me thinner all right, but the material was rough and the color, robin's-egg blue, too sweet. The white collar and cuffs made it look like a uniform. If I claimed I liked it and didn't wear it, she'd stand in front of my closet and say, "How come you begged me to buy that dress and now it lays?" Then I'd *have* to wear it. I took a deep breath. "I don't like it."

"What do you *mean* you don't like it? How can you not *like* it?" She stared. "Oh, I get it. It's *too* pretty. You *wanna* look ugly."

I studied myself in the mirror. My hair was parted down the middle and the sides hung straight: a reddish helmet with bangs. My face looked pliant, although my father said cheekbones were there, underneath. I looked at my plump, sexless body, and tears welled up. "The dress makes me look like an *usherette*. How come you want me to look like an usherette?"

She laughed. I brushed away the tears, but she saw them. "What are you *crying* about?" She cast admiring glances at herself in the mirror. She was wearing a red wool suit, with little weights in the jacket and skirt. It hugged her body perfectly. "What on earth have you got to cry about? A mother wants to buy her daughter a dress, and this makes tears? Silly girl. Take it off. I'm the last person in the world to force a child against its will."

I got dressed and we left empty-handed–as usual. My father chose most of my clothes, trading coats with other manufacturers for poodle skirts and fuzzy sweaters. "No one will have anything like that, kid," he'd say.

On the way home, we stopped at Waldbaum's and waited on a deli line that curled back and forth like a large intestine. "Pound of Nova, make it nice. Half of sturgeon, thin. Pound of corned beef, no fat," my mother said at our turn. Her voice was chalky, her eyebrows high. "What else?" I said pastrami. "Pound of pastrami. Something else?"

Ham was next to the pastrami and next to it bacon. "Bacon."

Her eyes narrowed. She turned to the deli man. "That's all." She threw our packages in the cart and wheeled it fast. "We're Jewish, or have you forgotten?"

"You eat roast pork in the Chinese restaurant every week. You won't let anyone have a bite."

"Pork is different. With bacon, all I see is pigs."

"Pork comes from a pig!"

"I don't want it in my house. Okay? I didn't ask to be a Jew." She said the word "Jew" as if it were something vile she loved, like roast pork. "If I'd had a choice I would have said, 'Make me a Rockefeller.' It's funny, Christians have hated Jews for centuries, but they can't wipe us out."

"Christians don't hate me."

Her lip curled. "They'd sell you down the river as soon as look at you."

"Why is that?"

"They can't stand it that Jews aren't Christians."

"*You* can't stand it that Christians aren't Jews."

"Listen, how 'bout if I drive you to mass. You love them so much, go live with them. It's fine with me."

I stuck out my tongue. She stuck out hers, and she pushed our cart to the checkout. After she paid, I wheeled the groceries to the car. She walked behind, exhaling smoke in quick huffs. At home, unpacking, she said, "English muffins in the bread box. Ice cream in the freezer."

"I live here."

"Only temporarily." She looked at the ceiling. "I hope." We finished in the kitchen, then sat in the den, my mother with the *Post* on her lap, me with *Of Mice and Men*. But she didn't read and she wouldn't let me concentrate. "We're going to the Plantation. You can order a big lobster. Wear the lilac, it's gorgeous." She picked at a dry patch on her elbow. She looked at the paper and put it down, then walked to the living room. "Julie, honey, come here." She was standing in front of the sliding glass doors. "Lower the umbrella, wouldja? It's blowing."

I went out to the patio. Low tide scented the air. She watched me, miming instructions. When I came in, she sat at the table, her face in her hands. "God, I hate this house." She rubbed at her elbow. "What's gonna become of her?"

I sat beside her. "Who?"

"*Madelyn.* Who else?"

"What *is* going to become of her?"

"What do you mean?" Her face twisted.

I made my voice even. "You just said it."

"I used a *phrase.* You pick on every word, like the FBI." She sighed, pulling my head to her chest. She looked at my hair. "I used to have your color." She pulled my head to her cheek, and I smelled her Arpège. I let my head fall into her neck, and she stroked my eyebrows. "I say a lot of stupid things. Nothing's going to become of her. I mean *every*thing's gonna become of her. What do I know? You think I know anything?"

On the way to the Plantation there was talk about Serge, although I wasn't supposed to hear it. I zipped into the front seat. My mother and sister sat in the back.

"Monday at two," Madelyn whispered.

"What's Monday at two?" I asked.

"Nothing you need to know." My mother crooned to Madelyn, "Oh, *Mama,* I'm so glad. Call me after, or should I come? No, go to Daddy."

"I'm gonna see Miller."

"*What?*"

"He's home for the holidays." Madelyn's voice was tight, pleading.

"Over my dead body."

"Then it was nice knowing you."

"He's the one *responsible* for all this."

"No one's *responsible,* and there is no *all this.*" Madelyn folded her arms over her chest.

"I'm warning you."

"*Daddy!*"

"Let her alone."

"I *did* and look what happened."

Madelyn cried. "You never leave me alone."

"No one's had more freedom!"

Madelyn sobbed.

"Cut it out," my mother said, but my sister kept going. Finally my mother put her hands in the air like a criminal. "Okay, okay."

Madelyn didn't stop.

"I'm *sorry*. Stop, please. It's only a date."

"That's what I was telling you."

My father lit a cigarette and leaned toward me. "Irving Singer came in from Judy Girl Togs. His stuff is gorgeous. I'm gonna bring it home Monday. You'll knock 'em dead."

"Thanks."

"You have to thank me for clothes?"

I snuggled against him. He dragged on his cigarette, then tossed it away. He steered with his left hand, encircling me with the other arm.

The Plantation was in Blackberry Bay, a posher town than Luna Island. When we walked through the door, Mr. Ponte, the owner, grabbed my father's hand. "Mr. Stark. How are you?" He bowed to my mother, then bobbed twice at Madelyn and me.

"Darling," my mother said, showing dimples. "You look fantastic." She covered her mouth. "Why not, with your millions."

Mr. Ponte jiggled. "I wish."

"Why? Someone else should make it? In my book, you're tops."

He bowed again, then snapped his fingers. "Leonard." A man with a mustache approached. "Show the Starks to Howard." We followed, my father guiding my mother, his hand at her elbow, his eyes toting the appreciative looks she corralled. Madelyn wiggled her ass. I looked on everyone's plate.

Like all the waiters at the Plantation, Howard, who was at "our" table, was a tall, distinguished-looking black man. He seated us, then leaned into my father's ear. "I have baby ribs."

"Lean?"

Howard screwed up his mouth. "Have I ever brought you *fatty* ones?"

My father raised his hands. "Excuse me."

"Maybe." He handed out menus.

My mother said, "A small steak, well done, fries crisp."

Howard nodded, turning to Madelyn.

"I'm not hungry."

"You'll eat some of my steak," my mother said.

"And my ribs," my father added.

A smile smeared her mouth. Howard turned to me.

"The jumbo lobster."

My father glanced at me, his mouth even. "How about some wine," he said to Howard. "You choose."

Howard left. A busboy brought raw vegetables, salads, and garlic bread.

"How come the wine?" my mother asked, chewing with her mouth open.

"I don't need an occasion." He leaned close to her. "Who ever thought I'd have so much?" He turned her pearls, so the sapphire clasp sat on her collarbone. He put his fingers through her hair, and she snorted. Howard uncorked the wine, and poured some in my father's glass. "I'm sure it's good," he said without tasting it, and Howard filled the rest of the glasses. My father clinked his against my mother's and kissed her on the mouth.

"Gowan, Hersch," she said.

He took her hand and leaned his forehead against hers. "The fall line, I've never seen such sales."

"Oh, tell, darling." Her eyes were wide.

"Big."

"How?"

He smoothed his hand over his mouth. "Quarter of a million."

"No!" She touched his cheek.

"We'll know the figures the next few weeks." He looked at Madelyn with dog eyes. "But that's not the important thing. My Madelyn is going to be great."

My sister batted her lashes. My mother lit a cigarette. "From your mouth to God's ear."

"Julie's going to be great too," my father said.

"Julie? We were talking about Madelyn." My mother inhaled her cigarette. "Where does Julie come in?"

My father pressed my thigh.

"Really, where does she come in? I need to be reminded of Julie?"

"Let it go," he said.

My mother dragged on her cigarette and stared into space. Madelyn dabbed a celery stick into cottage cheese, and my mother drummed her fingers on the table until Howard brought the food. My mother cut her steak in half and put a piece on Madelyn's plate. My father gave her five ribs. I didn't offer her anything.

The lobster looked beautiful, with its brilliant orange shell and white flesh. I ate the claws first, then ferreted out the meat in the torso, pulling off each leg, breaking it in pieces, sucking. I sucked the gills and ate the coral, piling the shells in a bowl. The shells looked beautiful, and I arranged them, varying the shades of red. By the time I got to the tail I was full, but I pulled out the dense meat in one lump. I dipped it in butter, eating, dipping, eating. When there was no more, I ran my fingers along the plate and licked them.

When I looked up, my mother was smiling. "Did you enjoy that, darling?"

I nodded. My stomach pressed against my clothes, but when Howard brought fruit and ice cream I ate them too. My father got the check and left a ten-dollar tip. He shook hands with Howard, while my mother eyed the money. As we walked, she put her arm around my waist, but I pulled away, getting to the car, claiming the front seat.

Driving home, Madelyn fell asleep on my mother's shoulder and Frank Sinatra sang on the radio. "Embrace me, my sweet em*bra*ceable you," my father crooned along. He tried to catch my mother's eyes in the rearview mirror, but she was staring into space. "I love the many *charms* about you," he sang, drawing my head to his cheek. "Don't be a naughty baby, come to Papa, come to Papa do." He squeezed my shoulder. "Wanna go to the track tomorrow?"

"*Yeah.*"

He squeezed me again, and I closed my eyes, seeing everyone milling, us standing by the railing, yipping as the horses whizzed by. I'd be wearing a suit like my mother's. My father would be dressed in gray silk. I'd seem to be older and thinner, and we'd keep winning. We'd win so much, we'd go to the city for a show and sleep at the Plaza. The next day, off to a museum and lunch at "21." I was imagining a club sandwich, fastened with a fancy toothpick, when my mother ruffled my father's hair. "What are you two plotting?"

She couldn't see his smile.

It poured the next day, and we didn't go to the track. Wednesday, my father told me that Madelyn's trouble was low blood pressure. "It's not serious, but it'll take time." By Friday, I was sure about Serge. Saturday, on the way to the city, I told him I knew. We were on the train. I was going to help sell coats. I thought he'd be angry, but when I said the name "Serge" he smiled. "Oh, darling, he's a genius. He knows everything. Madelyn needs help. He'll teach her."

"What?"

He put down his cards. We were playing gin on a newspaper spread across our laps.

"If I knew I could do it myself. Let me tell you something, a smart man knows what he doesn't know. Business, I understand. The rest? Ehh. Serge is brilliant. He speaks ten languages."

"Is she crazy?"

"She's confused. It's normal at her age."

"Then why does she need a psychiatrist?"

"A psychiatrist isn't just for craziness. He's for getting you what you want. Madelyn's too trusting, that's her problem. Serge knows what people are. It's like going to school, only for her better."

I looked at my hands. "What do I need?"

"To lose the baby fat. All a woman needs is a good figure and brains. The brains you got."

According to this formula, the females in my family weren't doing too well: my mother's brains were shot, my sister's were going, and I was fat.

"I'll lose it. You'll see."

When the train slowed, he hustled us to a door, and we shot ahead of the crowd. I was wearing heels, my first pair, and they struck the pavement with sharp little clops–sounds that made them seem headed somewhere exciting. We walked west along Thirty-fourth Street, past stores boasting "suicide prices." Foreign voices, bartering, wafted through open doors. My father caught the energy. I could almost see the air slicing his cheeks. On the corner of Eighth Avenue, he kibitzed about the track with the paper vendor. On Thirty-sixth Street he invited Cohen of Cohen's Deli to bring his daughter up for a coat.

We made our way to Thirty-eighth Street, rode the elevator to the tenth floor, passed through two steel doors, and entered a bright showroom that was sleek and modern. Along one wall was a row of banquettes, each with its own chrome light, angled like an insect. Here, buyers would write out orders, using "Darling Designs" pencils. "Sweetheart," my father would say to the female buyers. "Dearest," his partner, Woody Lee, would sing, encircling padded shoulders. I knew my father didn't mean it. In the place, his voice was smooth as custard, whereas it crackled when he flirted with my mother. He'd pat the hands of male buyers, as he "threw in" leather buttons and fur collars.

We hung up our coats in my father's office. His desk was strewn with fabric samples and order forms. Next we proceeded to the cutting room, my father looking absorbed. The cutters steered jig saws through piles of fabric so thick they looked like solid blocks. The pieces would next be trucked to the factory, in New Jersey, and finished coats would return to the place. The cutters called out, "Hey, sugar," and "Hey, sweetness" to me. "Good morning, Mr. Stark," they said to my father. On their walls, naked white and brown-skinned women smiled out, their breasts high, their asses turned provocatively to the camera. The patternmaker, Mr. Gardenia, held up translucent material that looked like the ghost of a coat waiting to be born. My father studied the pattern. "No one, but no one, works like this man."

In the stockroom, standing before rows of coats, my father looked like a contented farmer in flourishing acreage. Woody was there: a tall, blond man, a good deal younger than my father. My father had started the business during the war, then sold half to Woody. They were equal partners, but my father acted more like the boss. "Woody could charm anyone," my father would say, "and the beauty part is, they don't know he's operating." My father liked saying that Woody had gone to college and played football.

Woody was laughing with Fred, a salesman, and Juan, a shipping clerk. Woody kissed me. Fred and Juan said "Hi," and to my father, "Good morning, Mr. Stark." Juan didn't smile. He stamped out his cigarette, picked up the butt, and threw it in a trash bin, his eyes trained on my father, who was following his every move.

"I can't believe this one," Fred said. His smile lines were so etched, he seemed to be grinning all the time. "My Josh and you should get together."

"Sure," I said.

"His mother wants him to be an engineer. What is this, an engineer?"

I shrugged.

"You don't know? All right. But you know how to sell." He put his hand against his cheek and rocked his head. "This one could sell ice cubes to Eskimos. You gonna follow in your father's footsteps?"

"Nah," Woody jumped in. "What does she need with this? She's talented."

Fred's smile dimmed. "So what will you be?"

"A lawyer or an artist." The lawyer was for my father, who said I grilled people like one. The artist was for me. I liked to draw, and teachers made shows of my work. But neither ambition was real. When I tried to imagine the future, all I'd see was a figure in a backyard, hedge-clippers in hand, wearing a candy-striped apron and staring into space.

"And a wife," Fred said.

"I guess."

He slapped the air. "Wait a few years, you won't be guessing. But you're young yet. What do you need to think about marriage? Anyway, you got a rich old man to take care of you."

"This one can take care of herself," my father said. He never got more specific.

When the customers streamed in, it seemed we were in a movie: my father directing, Woody playing the sidekick. Fred's laugh rose above the din. Woody smiled, shook hands, remembered names. I sucked in my cheeks, trying to look older, and I talked up velveteen collars and satin linings. I told mothers their kids looked like "knockouts" and knelt to button little ones, squaring their shoulders, smoothing their backs, as my father had done a thousand times to me.

The customers, all women, solicited my father's advice. "The red's finer. Here, feel. I put these buttons on coats twice the price." Kids paraded before him. "It was made for her, you don't question perfection." When a sale was clinched, he wrapped the coat himself, blanketing it in tissue paper, placing it in a stiff box, tying it with twine and attaching a carrying grip. "Wear it in good health," he said, then added the money to a wad in his breast pocket.

At noon, when the place cleared, my father gave Woody his share.

"Thanks." Woody didn't count it.

"I wanna take Julie out." My father cocked his head.

"Fine. I'll stay."

"No. Fred can lock up."

"Go. I've got calls. Have fun."

My father smiled, and I kissed Woody. We got our coats, and my father counted out eight crisp dollar bills, one for each sale I'd made. I tossed them in my pocket, trying to imitate his nonchalance, but I couldn't keep my hands off them.

Downstairs, we hailed a cab, and my father gave the driver an address on East Seventy-fifth. "Surprise, darling. We're going to see Wolf."

"Really? Oh great." I bounced on my seat.

Wolf seldom visited Luna Island. I hadn't seen him and his family in more than a year. He and my aunt Nadine had two daughters, Brenda and Brett, a year younger respectively than Madelyn and me. The girls looked like their fair, blue-eyed mother, with nothing of their father's dark stirring looks. Brenda was snobbish and cold, Brett creepily tough. But they gleamed in their expensive clothes and stylish New York ways. And there was my vivid, open-hearted uncle. Around him, it was like having two fathers.

Wolf had owned an antique store on Broadway but during the past year had bought a brownstone. My parents had described the move as a gamble, and I expected to see a nervous Wolf. But when we entered his shop—now called a gallery—he was the picture of self-confidence, relaxing on a green velvet couch, his left arm around a striking young woman with lacquered nails and red lips. Her skin was porcelain fine, her hair cut in a chic bob. She held a glass of wine, her chin tilted toward him.

My uncle lunged at my father, his white smile gleaming against his tan. "Herschela, you look great." He threw his arms around his brother and nuzzled his cheek. He tapped my father's stomach with the back of his hand. "Still like a rock, takes care of himself." He pulled me into his arms. "Some heartbreaker." He darted a look at the woman on the couch. "Darling, my brother Hersch and my niece Julie." To us he said, "Corinne Burkhardt."

My father tipped his head and smiled charmingly, like he did in the place. Corinne and I said hello.

"Corinne has some collection of Chinese pottery," Wolf said. "I saw a vase in California I thought would drive her wild. The guy's sending pictures." My uncle put a bottle of wine in my father's hand and two glasses in mine. "Drink, talk to Corinne. I got something to show you." He sped into another room.

The old shop was larger, but some of its corners were dark and dusty. Here, polished chairs sat on plush carpets. Country scenes in gilt frames lined the walls, and ornate glass vases and brass lamps gleamed atop tables and buffets.

My father poured wine and lifted his glass at Corinne. "To the Chinese." He sipped, crinkling his eyes over the rim.

"Wolf can track down anything. They don't come any shrewder." She took a sip of wine, then smiled up sweetly. "What line of business are you in, Hersch? No, don't tell me, Herschel's the brother who makes coats."

My father pointed at me. "There's a piece of my work."

I was wearing a pink number that flared at the hem. My father made a twirling gesture, and as I turned, Corinne clapped.

"By the way," my father said, "your jacket's beautifully cut." She was wearing an emerald suit, with muttonchop sleeves and a nipped bodice. "Very becoming, darling. The color's terrific for you."

She smiled. How could she not?

Wolf came back with a rug over his shoulder. "This just

arrived, Turkish." He unrolled it near the couch. "Look at the pinks. Feel the weight."

Corinne stroked it like a cat. "Umm."

My father touched the nap, then flipped up a corner.

"The back is almost as beautiful as the front, no?" Wolf said.

"How much do you get for something like this?" my father asked.

Wolf shot him a look then glanced at Corinne. "Oh, don't make me think about that now. It's so beautiful. I just might keep it."

Corinne laughed. "He says that about every piece he sells me, and you know, I always fall for it."

"Wolf is famous for his charm. He was the one my mother *didn't* hock for money. He *had* it, but she didn't badger him for it. He was her favorite."

"What are you talking?" Wolf poked my father's shoulder. "He remembers what he wants. Mama used to say, 'Herschel's the one with heart.' She loved *him* best."

"She probably loved you the same," Corinne said.

"Or hated us the same," Wolf shot.

"Whatever, you both turned out fine."

My father and uncle laughed ruefully, shaking their heads the same way. They caught each other's expressions and shrugged simultaneously.

"Who needs to think about that now? It's all finished," my father said.

"Naah. It never is. We're vets from the same war, but the war goes on." Wolf pounded his chest.

"Not in me, my dear brother. In me, it's dead."

"Life's too short to argue." He rubbed his hands together. "The hell with all this. Let's do the town." There was always a point when my uncle got an idea. He'd organize an outing to the circus or to Rumplemeyer's for sundaes. There was never any hesitation between his notion and its execution. He'd make calls, order cabs, and my father's largesse would bob like a little rowboat in the wake of my uncle's need to please. "Okay, we have lunch at Delmonico's, then I take you to *My Fair Lady*. Later, we'll see."

Corinne clucked her tongue. My father whistled, keeping his eyes on the young woman. She wasn't much older than Madelyn, but she seemed more knowing, poised. There was something of the animal tamer about her, a woman used to roars and bared claws, who asserted her strength by seeming to defer. She glanced at her watch, pausing like an actress. "I can't think of anything I'd prefer than gallivanting with the Starks, but I can't."

My father's smile faded. Wolf darkened. "Why not?"

"I have to see my father." She made it sound like a chore.

"*Your father?*" Wolf bellowed.

She looked embarrassed. "I promised to have lunch with him. I don't oblige him that often." She cast me a look that said, "You know how it is." "Don't pout," she said to Wolf.

He drew up his neck, and his features shifted until he was handsome again. Corinne got her coat—a sable. Wolf held it, and as she slipped her arms into the sleeves she said, "I could come for the pictures on Thursday, after Serge."

I laughed. My father pinched my arm.

"Come Thursday, darling," Wolf said, sliding his hand along her back. Corinne kissed him on the cheek. He planted a light kiss on her lips, then released her.

" 'Bye," she said over her shoulder.

We watched her step into a taxi, then Wolf turned to my father. "You told her about Serge?"

"He's a psychiatrist," I piped in. "Madelyn's going to see him."

"That's right, sweetheart. Your sister's a lucky girl. This man has degrees, oy, who can count them? I think he knew Freud. Corinne's his patient. So am I. So is Nadine, and Brenda, and Brett."

The ground seemed to shift. A week ago, I hadn't known

anyone who saw a psychiatrist. Now I knew six people and all
going to the same man. The atmosphere felt close, like a hot-
house. But Corinne looked all right and so did my uncle. He'd
never been richer.

"Corinne has this *meshuggaas* with a father and stepmother.
You shouldn't know from it. Serge put her back together . . .
no, I should say *put* her together. Sent her to Morocco last year. I
was buying, and I looked after her." He smiled. "She sends me
her friends. They don't know what they want, so I tell them." He
rolled up the carpet and leaned it against the couch. "Come,
darlings." He draped an arm around my father and the other
around me. "Nadine's waiting."

"Then how come you wanted to go out?" I asked.

My father looked at the ceiling.

"A whim. You can't live by plans. What would life be like if
we always did? Do you know what the plan was for your father
and me?"

I shook my head.

"Live like rats."

"But what about Nadine?"

"I would have called." He patted my cheek. "Don't worry,
she doesn't live by the book either."

I didn't believe him, but I was sorry, all the same, we
weren't going to Delmonico's and *My Fair Lady.*

Wolf locked the gallery, and we walked up the front steps.
He rang the bell and Violet, a pretty black woman who'd worked
for my uncle for years, came to the door. In the past she'd worn
street clothes. Now she sported a uniform and lace hat. "How
you, Mr. Stark?" she said to my uncle.

"Terrific."

She tipped her head at my father and me. "How you, Mr.
Stark? Julie?"

"Fine," we answered.

"That good."

She held out her hand, and we gave her our coats. She

disappeared, and my uncle led us down a corridor that ended at French doors. He pushed them open, and before us spread a room out of a magazine. The tables were glass and steel. On the pinkish beige walls were canvases of splashes and drips. The fireplace was white marble, the bleached wood floors scattered with rugs–some made of fur, others of bright, woven wool. There wasn't an antique in sight.

My aunt was sitting on a white couch, amid a nest of pastel pillows, a white Persian cat in her hands. She wore a dress of creamy wool, and her skin looked as fair and soft as the material. Ash-blond hair was swept off her forehead, and her hairline looked unusually even–straight as the horizon. "My God, look at Julie. You were a little squirt the last time I saw you. You've got a figure, darling."

"I have?"

"Don't you know?"

"I'm fat."

"Gowan," my uncle said. "Thank God for a little meat." He shot a look at Nadine. There wasn't an extra ounce on her.

She raised her eyebrows and smiled, her usual indulgent expression. Nadine was from Atlanta and had the attentive, gracious manner many Southern women cultivate. She talked slowly, musically. She'd lived in New York for twenty-five years, but her accent was as thick as Scarlett O'Hara's.

My uncle stood close to me. I could smell his cologne. "I think you're gorgeous."

Feet clomped down the stairs, and my cousins appeared. Brett, aged eleven, looked more babyish than ever. A thumb was jammed in her mouth. But Brenda was astounding. A year ago, at fifteen, she'd been as plump as me, and deep dimples had pierced her chipmunk cheeks. Now, wraithlike arms jutted from a sleeveless sweater. Her eyes looked huge, her mouth too wide for her bony face. Wolf gave my father a "you-see?" look.

As kids, Brenda had courted Madelyn, having no use for me, and things hadn't changed. She eyed me contemptuously as I kissed her. Her skin felt cold. Her body was like a stone with a secret in its heart. She was carrying a book, *Freud's Case Studies in Hysteria.* "How are you, Brenda?"

She flinched. "My name is *Bliss.*"

"Oh."

She tossed her head at the couch. "*They* won't accept it."

Wolf put his palms up. "Honey, I keep forgetting."

"You do it on purpose."

"I don't, I swear."

"You feel rejected."

"I don't, baby, honest."

"Serge said so."

"He did?" Nadine asked.

Brenda/Bliss nodded emphatically. "You think I'm throwing away something you gave me."

"What?" my uncle asked.

"*My name.* Really, sometimes you can be so dense."

"Serge thinks we feel rejected? He never said that to me." Nadine sounded hurt.

"He doesn't tell you everything, obviously."

My aunt pressed her lips together, biting back a remark. "Right. That's right. But listen, honey, I'll try to remember. I promise."

"Me too, darling." Wolf sighed.

Violet entered. She tinkled a bell, laughing. "Lunch is served." Wolf tried to lift the cat off Nadine's lap, but it hissed at him. "What a way with animals," she said, laughing. She stroked her pet, which huddled closer to her, like a familiar standing guard. Then it took off.

We trooped behind Violet, winding through a maze of rooms, each more elegant than the one before. The dining room was lit by a crystal chandelier and furnished with silk-upholstered chairs and an inlaid wood table. Nadine sat at the head, Wolf and my father on either side of her; Brett and I were opposite each other, and Bliss was at the far end.

"I've got shirts for Pa, and handkerchiefs," Wolf said to my father.

Nadine leaned toward me. "Brett here has become quite a little rider." She pronounced it "ridah."

Brett neighed and began eating the first course: crab salad. Each plate was garnished with little pickles and radishes carved like roses. My aunt ate a bit of crab.

"Eat," Wolf said to her. "Why do you think she's like that?"

My father took Nadine's hand and smiled at Bliss. "Never mind."

Bliss stared at my father, like a deer transfixed by light. An odd thing always happened when my father and Wolf got together: they traded families. Wolf would claim me and Madelyn, like a coach with fresh recruits. My father would shield my cousins and make common cause with Nadine, because each of them had a difficult spouse.

"How is Thea?" Nadine asked.

"So, so."

"Maybe y'all should move back to the city, now that the kids are grown. There'd be more for her to do."

"You think *a place* is gonna make a difference?"

She nodded and met his eyes. "She could see Serge."

"She's always been nervous, too many fears. I thought she'd relax when she had children, or when the business took off." He shrugged. "It's not her fault. You think Wolf and I had it bad? Nothing in comparison to her."

"That's the point of Serge. He helps clear debris out of the past."

He rested his face on his hands. "She wouldn't hear of it."

"What if I called?"

"Would you? She admires you so much, you know."

"Oh, honey, I'm no one to admire. I'll just tell her what Serge does for me. I won't prod."

"You would never do that."

She laughed ruefully. "I don't suppose, sir, you've been talking to my darling husband."

"You don't prod me, sweetheart," Wolf said. "You make me murderous, just like a wife is supposed to. Marriage, what are you gonna do, Hersch?"

My father ate crabmeat. "Do I know? Do I have answers?"

Nadine stepped on a button in the carpet, and Violet returned with the next course: roast beef, baby carrots, and salad. For dessert there was lemon tart. Wolf dug into his food. Nadine ate lightly. Brett neglected her meat but took two slices of pie. Bliss pushed crab salad around her plate. When the roast beef came, she took a sliver and poked it with her knife, and when the pie was served, she put up her hand like a traffic cop signaling, "Stop." Her restraint was breathtaking. I craved it even as I hungered for everyone's leftovers and the crispy bits sticking to the platter. She was so *thin*. How did she do it?

When we finished Nadine rose. "I'll help Violet."

Wolf pulled her down. "It's not your job."

She went slack. Brett glowered. But then Nadine roused herself and began gathering dishes. Bliss studied her face in the mirrors that surrounded the room. She lifted her nose and pulled back her cheeks, which made her look even more cadaverous. She was still mesmerizing, and I wanted to ask for her secret, but as Violet and Nadine carried plates to the kitchen, she darted off.

"You're stuck with me," Brett said. "Come on." She had a way of bossing me that made me comply. When the four of us had played, my sister and Brenda had made me their slave, and I'd tried to exact the same tribute from Brett. She'd just dawdled behind, impervious to commands, and I'd wound up doing everyone's bidding. I followed her now, to a perch on the fourth floor, which had a slanted ceiling and a bay window with a view of the garden. The room was as plush and peachy as the rest of the house, but Brett's walls were covered with horses.

"They don't tell you anything," she said.

"They do."

"They didn't tell you about Serge. I *knew* Serge before you'd even heard of him. Don't worry. No one tells me anything either, but I find out." She sat on her bed. "You should like me."

"I do," I lied.

"Don't give me that. You think there's something special about Brenda, excuse me, Bliss. Well, she's just a jerk like us. She thinks *Madelyn* has all the answers."

"Madelyn did until she got weird."

"Everyone's weird when you get to know them. Know what I mean?"

I nodded.

"No you don't. You think I'm creepy and dumb, but I could teach you stuff."

"I'm *older* than you."

She eyed me like a specimen. "Get down on all fours. I want to see your carriage."

I shrugged. It was easier to placate her than try to outwit her. She straddled me, running her hand along my sides. She tickled me, and I giggled, rearing up, but she dug her knees into my ribs and cackled, "Bad lines." I threw her off, and she bumped her head on a dresser.

"You're mean," I said.

She rubbed her head. "I'll tell you a secret."

"I don't want to hear it."

"My mother has electrolysis."

"What's that?"

"You don't know? See? There's lots I could teach you. They take out your hair with needles."

"Why does she do *that?*"

"So her hairline is straight."

"Why does she care about that?"

"So she can be perfect." She sucked her thumb. "I'm a Mouseketeer."

I didn't know if she was riding me again. "You're dreaming."

"I am."

"No Mouseketeer is named Brett."

"I'm Darlene."

"You don't *look* like her."

"We wear makeup. No one's supposed to know."

"But you don't live in *California.*"

"I fly there every week." She glared.

I met her eyes. She was just a silly kid, after all. "Okay, next time I'll know Darlene is you."

"I need to get out of this house. Understand?"

"Yeah." But I didn't. Her house was luxurious, her mother gentle, her father rich, her sister thin. I kissed her goodbye, smelling leather. She waved from the top of the stairs, looking through the bars like a little criminal.

Downstairs, Nadine handed me a box from Bergdorf Goodman. "I missed your birthday, darling. Open it."

Inside was a cream silk scarf, woven with tiny gold threads. It looked like her. "It's beautiful."

"Let's see how it looks." She lifted the scarf from its tissue-paper nest and folded it with practiced hands. She slipped it around my throat, and I felt the softness, the expensiveness. "It's perfect." She stroked my cheek.

"Wear it in high spirits," Wolf said, pulling me into his arms.

⋔

"Do you believe the way they live?" I said on the street.

"What's not to believe?" My father's voice had an edge.

"Like royalty."

"It doesn't take *that* much money. Your uncle likes to live high. We could too."

I didn't think so. Our house was still so cramped Madelyn and I had to share a room. My father said he liked things easy to

care for, but I didn't think that was the reason. Something in him
wanted smallness, no room for the unexpected, for strangers
dropping in.

Maybe my father sensed my doubt. Maybe something else
was eating him. He acted sullen as we walked. We had to go back
to the place, because he'd forgotten a file. I waited in the showroom, but when he didn't return, I went to the stockroom, and
that's when I heard him arguing with Juan.

They were standing near a rack of coats. They had the same
compact build. My father's back was to the door, and he didn't
see me. Juan acknowledged me with a movement of his lip.

"The Macy's order goes out today," my father commanded.
He was standing no more than three feet from Juan, but he spoke
as if a chasm separated them.

"It doesn't have to. I wanna take my kids to the park."

"I pay you for a whole day. You have responsibilities. I pay
you plenty, better than anyone else would."

"They pay shit. You pay better shit."

"*Shit!* Do you know what I had to work for when I started?
Do you think anybody gave me an afternoon off?"

"They should have. You wanna be like them?"

"I need to hear this after what I've done for you?"

"I *earn* my money. We're ahead of schedule because I break
my ass."

My father's face went red. "Ingrate."

"You want gratitude? This is a business. You make all the
profits. I'm not someone in your family who needs to be grateful.
If I *were* in your family, you would give me the afternoon off."
His face softened. "Oh, have a heart."

My father went gray. *"I don't have a heart?* I don't have
brains to stand here arguing with you. Okay, I'm everything you
say, a bastard. Case closed. This is a sweat shop, and I want you
to *sweat.*" He turned, meeting my gaze. His face was a curtain of
anger. Juan put his hands on his hips and nodded "Okay," but
there was mockery in his eyes and a look of triumph on his face.

I'd seen my father angry many times. His skin would turn scarlet, and he'd shout and point. When I was little, he'd chased me to my room and spanked me with his belt. Always the crime had been ingratitude. My father would leave the room, and I'd examine the red marks on my behind. I'd want him to die, saying it out loud. I'd wish it so hard I'd get scared he actually would die, which would send me to him, past my mother's sympathetic face. I'd apologize, feeling no remorse, and at first my father would look hard. Then he'd take me in his arms and tuck me in his lap, and I'd rock there, wishing to be lulled past caring about his unfairness, lulled past hearing the voice in my head that harped, "You shouldn't give in." And I was lulled.

I stared at him. His eyes were slits, the corners of his mouth turned down, his lower lip jutting forward. He was trying to seem controlled, but he looked mean. On the road, in his early days, he must have felt like Juan. Now he wouldn't admit he'd ever been weak. Juan's crime was reminding my father of his past. My father didn't see that, wouldn't budge.

I shut my eyes and there were clouds, a billowing whiteness surrounding a dim figure. As it grew clearer, I saw it looked like Michaelangelo's *Moses*, a bust of which sat—much to Stuart's chagrin—in our living room. I was sure Serge looked like that head, complete with the little horns. Serge was behind Bliss's thinness, my aunt's house, my uncle's wealth. I held onto Serge as my father led me through the place, as we walked down Eighth Avenue. I held onto Serge while clutching the dollar bills in my pocket. Somewhere along the line, I'd rolled them in a ball. They were soft and moist now, almost in shreds.

Chapter 2

SERGE DID INDEED work wonders. My sister saw him five times a week and soon stopped acting morose. She wasn't her old self either, though. She had more confidence, dash. Mornings, she took classes at NYU and afternoons worked for my father. Officially she lived at home, but we didn't see her much. She stayed with Wolf and Nadine. That way, she was free of my mother's nagging but not really apart.

My mother saw Serge three times a week. He suggested she go to the New School, and she did, choosing a course on famous trials. The professor had a thick accent, but she stuck it out. Next, she took French literature. When she was assigned *Madame Bovary*, she read everything by Flaubert; the same with Stendhal, Racine, and Corneille. She saw the movie *School for Scoundrels*, in which a bumbler is taught one-upmanship by a rogue, and said the mastermind was Serge. She trusted him as no one else, and if she reserved any doubt she showed no sign of it.

I'd find her in the den, her nose buried in Swift, Conrad. She still fought with my sister, but now they screamed, "Serge says," and "Serge thinks." Serge was the invisible witness to which my mother appealed, but she didn't always get her way. If Madelyn was stuck, she'd call the doctor, then hand the receiver to my mother. My mother would nod, the yelling would stop, and my father would look content. He didn't see Serge in his office, but they talked on the phone all the time.

When I'd ask my parents questions, they'd say, "I'll ask

Serge." It was as if they stopped being parents and became children again themselves. I could see them on the shore waving, the way they did when I was swimming at camp, but they were too small to be of use.

I knew Serge was old. He came from Russia and had lived in France. My parents would talk of his escape, clucking their tongues and shaking their heads. My mother imitated his accent, emphasizing the guttural "ch" sounds, the way he merged "s" and "z" and "w" and "v." But my parents didn't connect the analyst with their own accented kin. To the contrary, their relatives seemed even lowlier than before.

The second summer of Madelyn's treatment, Serge guided her and six other patients on a trip around the world. I longed to meet him. A few months later my wish was granted. First, I was sent to Windsor, a prep school in Blackberry Bay. My father broke the news as we walked by the sound. "I heard about a terrific school. The finest people send their kids. Wanna take the test?"

"Yeah," I said, afraid I'd fail. But when we drove to the campus, I knew I had to go. The main building, a Federal mansion, was laced with ivy and crowned with gabled roofs. White columns guarded the doors, and all around rolled lawns and tennis courts. I described it to Amy—we'd stayed friends, as Madelyn predicted. She said, "Whatsamatter, Luna Island High isn't good enough for you?" and it seemed we really were going separate ways.

I looked forward to the classiness I'd take on—maybe not New York City dazzle, like my aunt and uncle had, but something on the way, taste and refinement. My first day at school, I spotted a girl like Bliss—a mysterious, powerful freshman named Janet Asher—whom I chose to imitate and adore. I would see her in class, poised and unflappable. She was, I quickly learned, the pivotal girl in the fastest clique. I didn't reach out for her friendship. I felt too backward at first. Everyone knew more than me, and everyone's grandfather owned a housing development or a department store. I moped. My mother noticed, and that's when Serge, in the flesh, entered my life.

"It's tough breaking into a new school. The subjects, the kids," my mother said.

I was at my desk. "I guess."

"You could talk to Serge."

"Okay," I said evenly, though my chest was pounding.

"He's a genius. If you don't respond, you'll be the first one he couldn't help."

So on a Thursday afternoon in early November, I took the train from Windsor to Penn Station, then rode two buses to Serge's apartment on Third Avenue and Eighty-fifth Street. I could hear every heartbeat, feel every cell throbbing. His front door was open, as I'd been told it would be. I took a seat in the waiting room and looked around. Oriental carpets were scattered on the floor and books overflowed the shelves. The apartment smelled of furniture wax and spices. It looked and smelled like Europe: the Europe where Big Ben chimed and people ate French bread in cafes.

A door opened and a handsome woman appeared. She seemed European too, something about her salt-and-pepper mane, styled casually, and the soft tweediness of her sweater and slacks. She smiled at me quickly and slipped out the front door. When I turned, Serge was standing in the doorway, a man in his mid-sixties, looking nothing like Moses and everything like Charles Laughton in his *Henry VIII* period. He wore a thick wool suit and a paisley cravat. His gray hair, which was long and combed off his forehead, crowned a large, round face, with small, scrutinizing eyes. He smiled, and I saw there could be warmth in his face, but its most powerful aspect was seriousness. He held out his hand. "I am Serge." I took it, and he ushered me into an office and directed me to a maroon leather chair. He lowered himself into a swivel seat behind his desk. "How can I help you?" he asked.

I didn't know what to answer. I just wanted what my
mother and sister were getting. "I want to learn," I bleated.

"Here, mostly you will learn about yourself." His accent
was indeed a jumble of Germanic crunches, Slavic slurs, and
French slides. But his voice was confident, full of patience and
irony. "Your job is to say what comes into your mind."

My mind was blank.

He looked in my eyes, and I felt he could see inside me.
"Tell me about school."

"Everyone's been there a million years, and all their clothes
have expensive labels, and their chauffeurs drive Bentleys.
There's this girl, Janet Asher, the richest and smartest. She
speaks perfect French and goes to Switzerland every summer.
She gets high marks, even though she never raises her hand.
When we play field hockey, she doesn't even care where the ball
goes."

There was a bowl of fruit on Serge's desk. He picked up a
banana and peeled it. "Why is she so alluring?"

"I told you."

"You told me what you see, not what you feel."

"I feel . . . that she doesn't need anything."

"Bentleys, Switzerland, labels, to you this is not needing? I
think you describe a girl needing many things, but maybe not the
things you need."

"Are you sure?"

"Never."

A space opened in my chest.

⇊

I believed Serge would be for me, my special ally. That he
could be for me and also everybody else in my family, even if we

weren't all for each other, didn't then strike me as a problem. All I wanted was to navigate Windsor and win Janet.

She was tall and attractive, feature by feature, with heavy-lidded gray eyes, straight brown hair, and a bobbed nose, a little too small for her face. She somehow missed being beautiful, but no one achieved the perfection of her monied look. The goal at Windsor was to dress with immaculate taste, in clothes that were unmistakably expensive, but to appear to be unconscious that others were computing your status. When Janet threw her dia-mond-clasped pearls in her locker, it looked like they meant no more to her than her lunch.

Actually, her lunch seemed more significant. Each morning, she'd stand in the locker room and fling the sack away, as if she could not bear to have it near her, this food. She was slender—though not reed-thin like Bliss—but she couldn't pass a mirror without giving herself a once-over or patting her stomach with disgust. She'd toss her lunch under a bench or on a windowsill, never in the garbage. She did not want to eat, that was clear, but she couldn't literally throw the food away.

"I'm stealing Janet Asher's lunches," I confessed to Serge during my third week of treatment. "I take them every after-noon."

"What does she bring?"

"Fried chicken, sometimes steak, always fruit and cookies." The chicken was crisp, the steak charcoal-broiled, the cookies chewy, the fruit juicy. I'd find Janet's bag, open it, and pretend I was only going to have a look. I'd unwrap the parcels and tell myself I'd only eat a little. But the food always tasted so deli-cious I couldn't stop. I'd eat fast, afraid someone would see. I'd take her lunch to the hedges bordering the campus. There I was far enough from the milling students to go unnoticed, yet near enough to watch Janet and her friends sitting in a circle near the freshman steps. Without food of her own, Janet would nibble from her friends.

"You eat your own lunch too?" Serge asked evenly.

"First."

"Why isn't it enough?"

That seemed a strange question coming from him, since he was constantly eating: fruit and salad, steak tartare and cottage cheese, hearts of palm and celery sticks–everything dietetic, but lots.

"I think about food all the time."

"Why do you say you are *stealing* the lunches when Janet throws them away?"

I shrugged. I was on the couch, and I heard crunching. An apple?

"What comes to mind when you think about stealing?" He pronounced it "shtealink."

I closed my eyes and twirled my hair. I let my mind roam and saw our block in Washington Heights and a stoop in front of a small building. "I was near to the A&P, little, maybe four. A boy had a ruler, a red plastic ruler." I sat up. "I hate this." He was leaning back. The buttons of his jacket strained across his belly. "Do I have to go on?"

He crunched on the apple. "What do you think?"

"That you're getting me to talk."

More crunching. I lay down.

"The ruler," he said.

"I asked the boy if I could see it, and he gave it to me. I measured the step we were on and his arm and my leg. Then I put it behind me and asked where he lived and what his father did. He told me, not catching on to my scheme, and when his mother came out of the store he ran to her, forgetting the ruler, which was exactly what I wanted to happen. I was thrilled, but then I got scared. I wanted to throw the ruler away, but I couldn't. I *had* to keep it. I buried it in my underwear drawer. Every so often, it would flash up between my panties and I'd feel sick. It must have gotten lost when we moved."

"To you, this is stealing?"

"I *made* him forget."

"Maybe he had ten rulers, and this was the puniest one. Maybe he was happy to get rid of it."

"You're just saying that to make me feel better."

"This too is a crime?"

I felt like kissing him, even though he was ugly and old, but I didn't think it was allowed.

It was easier to keep track of Janet during gym. There was something touching about her knock-kneed legs meandering across the playing field. I never lost sight of them, even as I bounded from the locker room, my hockey stick out like a lance, my breath turning white in the stinging air. Hockey wasn't my favorite sport, but I enjoyed the clatter and always lost myself in the effort to score.

When I played on Janet's team, I covered her territory, and after a while she drifted toward me at the lineup. Once, she slipped on a patch of mud and skinned her shin. She was laughing at her clumsiness as I gave her a hand up, and although it was evident she could walk by herself, Mrs. Buchanan, our gym teacher, asked me to take her back to the locker room. I didn't object and Janet didn't protest, but I felt a pang of resentment for the license she claimed and everyone, including me, afforded her.

She came to my aid too. In French, I'd turn stupid, my tongue becoming thick like a cow's, and Janet would hiss answers, although we didn't fool our teacher, Dr. Prescott, who'd sniff and glare. Janet was unfazed. I tried imitating her bravado, but Dr. Prescott scared me, and, secretly, I admired her.

She was the object of mockery, because she was dowdy and ancient. The students could hardly choke back laughter when she wore, as she frequently did, a dress adorned with mink tassels, which bobbed on her broad bosom as she jabbed the blackboard and shouted, *"Formidable."* I was attracted to Dr. Prescott's indifference to fashion, even as I coveted Janet's style. The teachers at Windsor were poor. While the students sported costly new wardrobes, the faculty made do with frayed suits and dresses.

Dr. Prescott seemed beyond these petty struggles. She championed civil rights and defied other pressures to conform. She was oblivious of her own looks and of ugliness in general, particularly of the exceeding homeliness of Miss O'Neill, the tiny, gaunt woman who taught in the lower school and with whom she shared an apartment. I knew they were lesbians, and I took Dr. Prescott, with her commanding manner, to be "the man." I could not picture them in bed, but it didn't matter. It was enough that they were unconventional.

I myself wasn't ready for such independence. I joined the Booster Club because Janet was in it. The sole purpose of the Booster Club was slicing oranges for the boys' teams, and standing in the kitchen beside Janet, with knife in hand and a tray of fruit before me, I felt like an initiate to a new order.

Our first outing was serving the basketball team. I waited on the sidelines, pretending to care who scored, and at halftime carried my tray to the players, adopting Janet's pigeon-toed walk. The boys, their hair slicked with sweat, wolfed down the fruit, thanking us, and I felt myself switch into flirt gear. I turned it off, thinking it wasn't civic-minded. Then I noticed what Janet was doing. Her hands were fluttering from the oranges to her hair. She giggled for no reason and brushed her breasts absently. She blinked and commented on the boys' plays. I found it amazing that she understood basketball so well when she continually forgot the rules of field hockey.

Taking her cue, I said to no one in particular, "It was great the way you dribbled between your legs," and a bulky senior named George Norton said, "Thanks."

Janet stared at me, and as the boys lumbered back to the

court, she gasped, "He *liked* you. God, I can tell." She studied
me. "You like them, too, don't you?" I wasn't sure if this was a
compliment, but I smiled, smelling sweat and oranges, feeling
the weekend energy. She touched my arm, the smallest gesture.
"Come to my house. Eat dinner and spend the night."

"*Yes,*" I said. "But I don't have any sleeping stuff."

She smiled. "I've got tons."

Then I ate three orange sections in a row.

Janet's chauffeur was named Miles. Miles drove a silver
Rolls-Royce. Sitting in the sedan atop soft leather seats, Janet
acted like she was in a school bus and I gazed out the window
like the Queen of England. We drove through lush estates, then
turned onto a tree-lined drive, at the end of which sat a colonial
mansion, with eight thick columns. Miles deposited us at the
door and drove to the garage. I took a deep breath, inhaling
privacy I'd never known.

Janet gave me a tour. The grounds receded in terraces that
graded to gardens, a swimming pool, tennis courts, and a dock
which, in summer, I was told, held a fleet of boats. In the center
of the main house curled a romantic staircase. The carpets, the
sofas, the walls above the paneling, the ceilings and moldings
were all in earth tones: tans, grays, and greens. The place was
quiet, except for the nails of the golden retriever, which clip-
clopped on the marble floors.

The dog's name was Martin. The cook's name was Hester.
That night, Hester served her "famous fried chicken," and when
Mrs. Asher asked how I liked it, I said it was "zesty" and flashed
one of Janet's gracious smiles. I wasn't about to say that I adored
Hester's chicken, that I probably ate more of Hester's chicken
than anyone else in the world. There it was, all crackling and
steamy on a silver platter—the original of what I knew so well in
its foil-wrapped form. I felt mocked by the chicken, but it was
also titillating. I had a secret unknown to the Ashers. I knew the
complete life cycle of their fried chicken.

Mrs. Asher was tall and slim, with a worried look around her

hazel eyes. Mr. Asher was handsome, with black wavy hair–
better-looking than either his wife or child–but he had the family
haziness, unease coupled with an attempt to hide it, a look of
puzzlement that discontent should have cropped up amid so
much material comfort.

Janet took a breast from the platter, cut into it, and chewed,
as if she ate like this all the time. "We lost the game," she said
between bites, her tone flat.

She did not meet her parents' eyes, and I thought she was
sulking. Before dinner, Janet's father had kissed her on the cheek.
He'd held her by the shoulders, releasing her when he was done,
and she'd shrunk back. It had happened quickly, a father-daugh-
ter moment that could have signified nothing.

"The boys always lost in my day too," Janet's mother said.

"I was one of those boys." Janet's father smiled ruefully.

They went on sending up desultory remarks, like lonely
weather balloons. I thought Serge would have been bored. I
would have been too had I not been on the hunt for secrets. I was
hoping Janet's parents would say where their money came from
or how it felt to be rich. They didn't ask what my parents did.
They didn't ask me any questions, and I didn't know whether I'd
failed to engage them or if they just weren't interested in people.
In any case, it was going to be up to me to steer the conversation
to money, and I was planning to, by admiring their things. But as
coffee was served Janet rushed us from the table, and at that
point, all I'd learned about the Ashers was that they made dull
conversation and all they'd learned about me was that I liked
Hester's chicken.

Janet led me to her room–really a suite, with a sitting area
and separate sleeping space. There was a bathroom and dressing
room, with double doors leading to a closet. I wanted to open it,
but Janet pulled me away, promising to show it to me later. She
sprawled on her bed, leaning on pillows, dangling her shoes until
they clattered to the floor. She patted a place for me and said,
"My grandfather got rich importing wine."

I adjusted a pillow behind my neck, startled she could read me so well.

"My father just plays with the money on the stock market. And as for my mother, she was married to another man first. I heard it from my aunt Lenore. Can you believe it?"

"No," I lied.

"Can you believe all that secrecy?"

"Well, yeah."

"Just to keep me from knowing she'd had sex with another man? God, she's had sex with every salesman in Blackberry Bay." When Janet said "sex," Martin jumped on my lap, turned on his back, and exposed his floppy parts. I rubbed his belly, and maybe that's what gave Janet the idea I was familiar with male anatomy. She sidled up close. "Beach kids are fast, aren't they?"

I shrugged and kept rubbing.

Janet's eyes followed my hands. "Did you ever see one?"

"What?"

She pointed to Martin's privates. "On a boy."

I nodded. I'd sighted my first penis over the summer.

Her eyes glittered. "Tell."

"There's this guy Jerry, sort of a boyfriend. He goes to my beach club. Anyway, one day, he was waiting for me by the pool and he had his legs up on the diving board, and as I got close, I realized his stuff was hanging out."

"What did it look like?"

"Purple and lumpy."

"How can you tell the penis from the balls?"

I looked at Martin. "The balls have hair on them. But you know, I only got a flash. Jerry stood when he saw me, and I felt creepy and dizzy. He was talking, and I kept saying, 'Huh?' because I was thinking, 'Here's this cute guy, with all this *stuff* under his clothes.' And when I knew what it looked like, I couldn't get it out of my head. Know what I mean?"

She shook her head slowly. "No, and I don't think I want to. What's the big deal if it's so awful-looking?"

"Maybe it was the angle. Maybe it looks better standing up."

Janet giggled.

"I mean when *the boy* is standing up."

She threw back her head and laughed, and I thought we'd be friends. Not like Amy and me, because I couldn't imagine feeling that close to Janet, but we'd keep surprising each other. Light glinted on her teeth. She petted Martin's head, and we talked as if we already were friends, describing the way boys got hard-ons when they danced with you, and how their palms got sweaty, and how you sometimes had to push their heads off your shoulder. Mostly Janet asked questions and I talked, and I got the feeling that maybe beach kids *were* faster.

"He put his *tongue* in your *mouth?*"

"It's not so bad, compared with other stuff."

She closed her eyes, trying to picture Jerry and me soul kissing under the boardwalk. "How do these things happen?"

"Something makes you want them to touch you, and you concentrate, and then they do, and you feel this power, like you can make the things in your head come true. Of course you have to *want* the boy to do stuff or the feeling doesn't come."

Janet sighed. "Of course."

I eyed her slim form, and air escaped me too.

She pulled up her legs. "I've never willed anything. Things just happen. Windsor, Europe, things." She rattled off the countries she'd visited, and I saw her crisscrossing Serge's Europe.

"The Tower of Pisa *really* leans?"

"Does it! You can't believe it's not going to fall."

"What keeps it up?"

She smiled. "We keep coming back to that question."

I laughed. "What's Venice like?"

"Beautiful: the water, the light, the clouds, the sea. You feel the oldness, nothing like here. We go every year."

I twirled a piece of hair. "How can you bear to come back?"

"You get tired after a while."

"But why? Europe sounds so much more exciting."

"It's just different. You can get tired of anything."

But I didn't think I would. I pressed her for more information, and she said she could order dinner in five languages, which seemed a waste, given her usual indifference to food. She was describing first-class accommodations on the *France* when she yawned and looked at her watch. "Let's get you a nightgown." She went to her closet and opened the doors, casually, and I looked inside. I thought my eyes would fall out of my head. The space was as large as my bedroom, with rows of coats, dresses, skirts, blouses, and sweaters. Everything looked new. From the bed, it was hard to make out individual things, but the abundance was overwhelming. The shoes were in the center, on a tiered stand, and in the center of the display were Janet's twelve pairs of Pappagallos loafers, each a different color. I'd noticed these shoes during my first days at Windsor. They were made of the softest leather and had thin little soles. The most alluring girls wore them, walking with a shuffle that said, "I can kick anything out of my way." I'd put them out of my mind, thinking they must cost way more than my mother would spend. But seeing them now, all twelve pairs, I had to have at least one. "Where do you buy them?" I pointed.

"What?" She sounded vague.

"*Those.*"

I moved toward the closet. She looked at my face, plucked a nightgown off a hanger, and shut the door before I could get in. "I get mine in Panache, on Hudson Mews. My mother likes them because they fall apart easily, and that way she can buy more. She flirts with the salesman. He has a mustache. You would probably like him too."

She gave me a nightgown made of powder blue satin; it had lace trim and spaghetti straps. She undressed without embarrassment, maybe even flashing her body, and slipped on a cotton gown. She'd given me the sexier one. By accident or on purpose? I took off my clothes and slid the gown over my chest and hips. I looked in the mirror, seeing my helmet of hair and tawny skin, but also a creature in a magazine.

That night I dreamed I was walking through our house on Luna Island, when all of a sudden I saw a corridor I'd never noticed before. Passing through it, I came to a large kitchen, the floor of which was strewn with a rainbow array of petrified fruit and vegetables. They looked like jewels, and as I bent to gather them, I discovered a secret staircase off to the side. I climbed it slowly, apprehensively, clutching the banister. But at the top was a series of spacious, airy rooms, with brick walls, lustrous wood floors, and furniture upholstered with intricately patterned material. I was amazed and happy, until I felt a cold draft. I looked up, seeing that the roof was missing, and felt afraid a thief would drop in. As I stood there, however, no one came. There was no one but me, and when I looked up again, the sky was thick with stars.

*

"How did you feel when you woke up?" Serge asked.

"Excited and worried."

"What was the worry?"

"That my mother would be angry when I told her I wanted the shoes."

"Perhaps you were also worried that Janet would be angry. Perhaps you feel that the shoes are not rightfully yours, like the lunches and the ruler."

Serge had a way of rushing me to see things. It felt like my eyelids were being pried open.

"I will give you an interpretation of the dream, and we will see if it fits, like a glass slipper." He chuckled. "You are attracted to this girl, because she is rich and powerful, but she does not seem to have much of a heart, so she asks you to tell her about feelings. You think the things she knows are very important, and you do not think the things you know matter very much. Now, in the dream you find a strange kitchen with fruits. You also said they look like 'jewels.' Say the word out loud."

"Jewels, jewels. I don't get it."

"Shush, relax, try again."

"Jewels . . . jewels. Oh I see, Julie. But what does it mean?"

"You feel a strong connection to these objects. Let's say the kitchen represents your school. Remember the kitchen where you cut oranges? But these fruits are all different colors. To me, they suggest both Janet's shoes and her lunches."

"What about the fruit *you* eat?"

"Very good. My food is surely something else you want. But just as you are finding the fruit, you see something that makes you leave it. You discover rooms upstairs that you did not know existed. Close your eyes, and tell me what comes to mind."

I stretched my limbs like a starfish. Janet's closet flashed into view. "When Janet opened her closet, it was like discovering a room."

"Good. Remember, too, that Jerry's penis was something you *discovered*, even though it was there all along."

I felt clammy. "What does it mean?" I whispered.

"We are getting there, don't worry. I am struck by the way the rooms upstairs look, the furniture. You say there are designs on the fabric. What do they suggest?"

I didn't know, but on the wall in front of me was an oriental carpet. I stared at it, as I often did, losing myself in the patterns. I pointed. "The furniture belongs to you! But what does *that* mean?"

"I am teaching you to use your intelligence. Upstairs, those are the pleasures of the mind. They feel unsafe to you, because you are not sure you are entitled to this knowledge–like knowing what is in the closet and seeing the penis. In other words, what is inside a woman and what a man has. That is why you imagine a thief, which, of course, is only yourself. In the end, however, you are more adventurous than afraid, and that is the way you must be with Janet. You are not stealing those shoes. They belong to you as much as her."

"Thanks."

"Thank yourself. The dream comes from you. It all comes from you."

⚜

I told my mother about the Pappagallos, explaining they cost twenty-eight dollars.

She rose up clear. "All the kids have them, and my child feels left out? Not on your life. What's money for?"

We went to Panache, in Blackberry Bay. My mother—who tended to wear one pin or scarf too many—wasn't as chic as Mrs. Asher, but she was prettier. The salesman with the mustache admired her sweater. She smiled. I chose red shoes, and she didn't object.

⚜

"Two triumphal snatches," Serge said, comparing the shoes to the ruler.

At school, I flaunted them like trophies. Walking across campus, my feet looked like actors. I knew the rule at Windsor was never to wear the same item twice in a row, but I loved the shoes too much to comply. I wore them every day, scuffing the heels as I flirted with punks at the train station.

I began to grow into them. I spoke up in French, and Dr. Prescott said, *"Formidable,"* her mink tassels bobbing. I asked

Serge to help me catch up with the others. "Ya, ya," he said, giving me Shakespeare and Donne, Dickens and Melville, Hardy and Mann. There was a lot of exciting talk in these books about right and wrong. Since all the authors were Christian–as were Dr. Prescott and her cohorts–and since the Jews I knew only talked about need and desire, I got it into my head that morality was gentile. When I thought of being good, there came washing over me the most delicious sensation of being bad.

"Bullshit," Serge huffed, giving me a biography of Herzl. Next came Marx, Trotsky, Goldman, and Luxemburg, as well as books about Hitler and the war. Serge didn't talk about his own peril. To the contrary, he stressed that Jews could negotiate the world, master fine distinctions, be included in everything.

Janet made a point of walking with me from French to gym, when we'd discuss Jacqueline Kennedy and "The Twilight Zone." "I always guess the endings," she'd say. She didn't comment on my Pappagallos. I assumed she was being discreet, for to acknowledge them was to note that I once had not possessed them and, in fact, still lacked all manner of things thought essential at Windsor. At lunch, she'd sometimes pull me into her circle. It made me giddy but nervous, for on those days I couldn't get to Hester's food and I was afraid Janet would deduce that I was the secret eater. She knew there was one, I was sure. Yet despite her attentions, the camaraderie I'd felt at her house didn't recur.

It was disappointing. Her authority and restraint kept me watching, wondering, and I hovered in her orbit, neither, strictly speaking, inside nor out, until the April dance. I brought Jerry, the boy whose private parts I'd glimpsed, and it turned out to be the smartest move I'd made at Windsor.

For the dance, the lunchroom was decorated with mermaids and fishermen. No one noticed Jerry and me when we arrived, but once we started dancing, I could feel attention gathering. Jerry's arms were bare, and his pants hugged his thighs. His hips jutted rhythmically, and his feet wove graceful patterns. I caught his freedom—I knew it wasn't coming from me, or maybe it was. "Shake it up, baby," the Isley Brothers shouted, and we shook. "Do you love me?" the Contours asked, and we bounced and gyrated. I watched Jerry's face grow rosy and damp, and when a drop of his sweat hit my lip, I licked it. There was heat between us, heat in our smiles and hands. There was heat all around, and it permeated the room.

The girls devoured Jerry. The boys moved in on me as if I'd become sleek and beautiful. I danced with boys whose names I didn't catch, whose faces I couldn't place. I danced with boys who stepped on my Pappagallos, but I didn't care.

When I finally rested, I saw Janet. It struck me as odd I hadn't thought of her before. She was watching her friends dance. She looked beautiful, more elegant and shimmering than anyone in a silver and cream dress that must have cost a fortune. She didn't acknowledge me, and, for the first time, I didn't approach her either. Instead, when Jerry sat down, I asked him to ask her to dance.

"Sure," he said, and walked off with his rolling, cocky gate. He tapped her on the arm, and she smiled. As they moved onto the floor, the music grew slow, and Jerry took her in his arms and held her against his body. I wondered if she feared she might arouse him and, if she did, whether it would disgust her. I'd talked about Jerry and now produced him in the flesh. Janet and I would laugh. So would Jerry and I.

When the music stopped, Janet stood with her head cocked, and I thought she was willing Jerry to stay. He took her hand and steered her across the floor. She didn't know where they were headed, but when she realized it was toward me her face twisted. It was the look she wore when she threw her lunch away. She turned her back and stood still. She just stood in the middle of the floor as the next song started, and I thought of dancing with her myself, to reassure her. But just then bulky George Norton approached, and she fell into his arms. I told Jerry I was tired, and we drove home. All the way, I felt a dull dread.

On Monday, Janet didn't ask me to eat with her, and I didn't see her lunch. After hockey practice, I couldn't find my Pappagallos. The shoes weren't under the bench, where I'd left them, or in the lost-and-found. They weren't anywhere.

Janet wore them the next day. I spotted them on her feet as she passed me on the stairs. I knew they were mine. Hers were pristine, while my toes had left impressions in the leather. When I saw my shoes on her feet, I wanted to slap her, but I couldn't even speak. She acted like I was invisible, and for the rest of the day I could not look at her face. My eyes went automatically to her feet, like a serf.

※

"Look at the poetic irony," Serge said. "You stole her lunches, she stole your shoes. You could say you are even."

"She threw her lunches away. I *loved* my shoes."

"Anything you get is garbage, and everything that she does is powerful. That is not the whole story. You pitied her, so you could show off your success with boys. You were devious, and she got angry. She's entitled."

"She wanted to take Jerry away."

"This, you do not know. All you know for sure is that you showed off."

I felt warm.

"Janet reminds you of your mother, because she is slim, as you wish to be. She prefers other females to you, just as you believe your mother favors Madelyn. When you sent Jerry to dance with her, you were acting out a wish to show your mother that your father prefers you. You cannot succeed with your parents, because your father frustrates your desires. With Jerry and Janet, you got your wish and you thought that it was so bad you let her keep your shoes. It was not so bad. You just did it. And Janet is not so powerful. You just believe it."

"So what do I do?"

"What do you want?"

"My shoes."

"Then get them."

"How?"

"I do not think you will find them outside your door, carried there by elves. Open your mouth."

Janet wore them the next day, and during lunch I caught her in the locker room. "Those are mine." I pointed at her feet.

Her lip curled. "What are you talking about?"

"I left my shoes under this bench, and now you're wearing them."

"These are *mine*. What would I need yours for?" She met my eyes.

"I don't know. You tell me."

"These are my shoes. I'm sorry you lost yours, but there's nothing I can do." She walked to her locker and took out her lunch. She tossed it to me. "Here. I know how much you like Hester's chicken."

I caught the bag. "I want my shoes." I threw the lunch at her, and it hit her in the chest, then fell to the floor with a meaty thud. I moved closer. "Put them under the bench tomorrow. It can be our secret."

Her face went hard. "I don't have any secrets with you."

"You're a thief."

"Takes one to know one." She tapped the lunch with her foot, then picked up the bag and threw it in the garbage. "You're strange, really strange. I guess beach kids are like that." She moved toward the door.

I grabbed a hockey stick from the rack and blocked her way. "What's wrong with strange?" I pointed the stick at her feet. "Take 'em off."

She feinted, breaking for the door. I swatted at her feet, making her hop.

"*Stop that.*"

"Give me the shoes."

"No."

I charged, knocking her to the floor. Her legs splayed awkwardly, but, miraculously, the shoes stayed on her feet. I tried to get them off, but she wrestled me away. As we rolled, I could smell her perfume, see freckles around her nose and red strands in her hair. She got the upper hand, straddling my stomach, pinning my arms. She shouted, "My legs are ugly. My mother screams at Hester all day. My father poses in front of the mirror."

I stopped struggling. "Your legs aren't ugly."

"What do you know?"

"Why does your mother scream?"

"She's bored and angry."

"Why does your father pose?"

"He's vain and shallow." A series of emotions swept her face. "He's not really my father. Oh, I don't know."

"How can you stand to starve?" I asked, and her emotions settled into contempt.

"I *don't* starve. Sometimes I don't want to eat. I'm bored with Hester's food, but it goes on, day after day." She screwed up her mouth. "You have to stop looking at me."

"I'll stop looking if you give me back my shoes."

She stood, gazing at her feet. I caught her eyes, willing her to comply, but she shook her head. "You'll keep looking no matter what. You can't help yourself." She brushed off her clothes. "No deal."

✣

"Such things happen in a rich school?" Pearl, my mother's friend, said. We were in the kitchen. Strands of chestnut hair were escaping her upsweep. She put her arm around my waist. "You weren't meant to have them."

"That's a way to figure?" my mother shot.

Pearl tucked up some tendrils with a hairpin. "That way there's less disappointment."

"Never mind. Better she should risk it. Expect everything, my darling daughter. Tomorrow, we'll get another pair. What? My kid should be heartbroken for thirty dollars?"

"Twenty-eight."

"That's criminal. Next time, you better lock them up. Waste, I can't take. It goes against my grain."

✣

"It's funny," I told Serge. "I don't feel bad."

"You got under her skin. That was even better than getting into her closet. You saw there was nothing so special in her you lacked. As a bonus, maybe her family is even crazier than yours."

As I heard these words, I felt a security that seemed new. I thought Serge was preparing me for something wonderful. Windsor was just the start.

"Perhaps you are not sad about Janet," he said, "because you are imagining the bigger fish, with bigger secrets, you have yet to catch."

Chapter 3

JACQUES WAS MY next fish, Jacques, Madelyn's boyfriend. I discovered him after my teen tour. My parents had vetoed Europe, saying, "What will you have to look forward to if you go now?" They'd thrown me the Rockies instead, and over the summer, I'd gone off with new friends, a bunch who appreciated Dr. Prescott and considered Janet's clique shallow. These girls read Kafka and Sartre. Saturdays, they prowled Greenwich Village, forcing down espressos. I did too.

While I was away, Madelyn and Bliss rented an apartment—a sunny place on East Sixty-fourth Street. Corinne's father, who was in real estate, found it. Wolf supplied the furniture. Madelyn also met Jacques.

"He's an artist," she said, grabbing my hand and tugging me into her room. Her hair was short, boyish but glamorous, and her nail polish and lipstick matched, like Corinne's. They'd become friends—through Serge or Wolf. "Look." Madelyn pointed to a pastel portrait: a woman in a magenta kimono. It was my sister, and yet it wasn't. The artist had caught the shape of her face and her tawny coloring, but he hadn't painted her quality of ready amusement. The eyes were masked, almost blank. It was as if another woman had been superimposed.

"You look Japanese."

"Jacques says I'm exotic. He made me wear the robe."

I plopped on her bed. "How'ju meet?"

She sat beside me. "Ballet."

"He dances?"

"He plays the piano. That's how he makes money." She leaned on a pillow. "Get this, he comes from Paris, he's thirty, and he's not Jewish." She flashed her dangerous smile. "I did it."

I stared at her. She was riding in a different orbit now. "*Tell.*"

"Jacques loves women, *knows* them."

"What is there to know?"

"Places, feelings."

"How do you know you have them?"

She hugged herself. "You find out with the right man."

"How do you know you have the right man?"

"The way they look at you, like they can't get enough."

"What does *that* feel like?"

She ran her hand through my hair. "You'll see." She propped herself up and studied the portrait, tilting her head as if trying to match it with some idea of herself. "Do you think I'm bad?"

I shook my head. "You're really living."

"Mommy and Daddy would die. Don't say a word."

"When have I ever blabbed?"

"I told Serge."

"Well, sure," I said, bothered that the confidence had been shared. "Remember when we used to play flying angel?"

"Of course."

"Do you do it with Bliss?"

She shoved my shoulder. "Get out of here. Her hipbones would cut my feet to shreds." She stroked my hair. "Don't be jealous."

"I'm not!"

"You always are."

I sighed.

"You'll have your turn."

"Everything will be used up by then."

"Flip over, and I'll do your back."

I stretched out, and she hitched up my sweater. Her hand

moved across my skin, a perfect combination of tickle and scratch. She drew a picture, and I made out a face with glasses. The mouth was straight, something flowed at the neck . . . a scarf. "Do it again."

She did.

"It's Serge!"

She laughed.

"It's Serge, isn't it?"

She kept laughing.

It was Jacques. He was at Madelyn's the next time I came, a slim, handsome man, about five feet ten. He wore tight jeans, a shirt open at the neck, and a small, knotted scarf. Light brown hair waved across his forehead, and wire-rimmed glasses perched on his nose. He spoke with only a slight accent, working hard to pronounce words properly. Madelyn was eager for me to like him, since I was the only one in the family allowed to know him. I'd visit them after Serge, and we'd eat dinner, see a movie, or talk.

Jacques was sexy. My uncle Wolf was too, but he didn't act like he needed women. For Wolf, flirting was a sport or a gamble; he used the same words and moves over and over. Jacques's style was closer to my father's. He remarked on women's clothes and breathed them when he kissed. But my mother didn't respond to my father the way Madelyn did to Jacques. She touched him, taking the lead. It was the sort of freedom she took with me, but with Jacques there were deeper currents. Her body stiffened and relaxed more.

I'd watch them in the dimness of movie theaters, their arms around each other, their legs entwined. Sometimes, Jacques would turn to my sister, not speaking, studying her profile. She'd hold her head steady, although an eyebrow might twitch. On the street, she'd grab his belt, tugging him to a shop, and he'd bounce along amiably. He'd hold scarves against her skin, picking colors for her complexion. At makeup counters, he'd have her try different lipsticks, then choose the shade he thought best.

He was emotional, like my father. But my father could talk freely only about love—whom *he* loved—while Jacques could show sadness too.

I saw this one night in the Tokyo Moon Restaurant, when Madelyn asked why he'd come to the States. He looked at his teacup and said, "A woman."

"That figures."

He waved his hand. "A long story."

My sister stopped eating. Her body was full of quiet and trust, except for her neck, which was arched. "Tell it."

He mixed mustard and soy sauce in a little dish, dipped raw fish in the concoction, and offered it to Madelyn. She opened her mouth and chewed, and he said, "Her name was Rivette. We met during the war, when she was a little girl, seven. She was a Jew." He scanned our faces, looking for some recognition. We sent back our usual blankness. "Her parents were killed in a concentration camp, but she survived and came here. She wrote to my parents, and afterward I visited her."

"What did she look like?" Madelyn asked.

"Long red hair, dusky skin, a pointed face."

The woman in the painting, I thought.

"How did you meet her?"

"She lived next door. Her parents were poor but cultivated, lots of books, from Poland. My parents gave them food. We owned a small *boulangerie*, and to pay us back, Rivette's mother taught me to play the piano. I taught Rivette to speak French. I was the one who gave her the name Rivette—her real name was Rivka. She learned quickly, a little show-off with her Parisian accent, talking for her parents in shops and on the Metro." He

shook his head, and a wave of hair fell across his eyes. "When the
Nazis came, her parents went South and she stayed with us. She
could have spent the war in Paris, safe. She was like a little sister.
We slept in the same room. But she was afraid her parents
wouldn't get by without her, so she went to Lyons. By the time
she arrived, they had already been sent to Auschwitz."

Madelyn shoved a piece of tempura in her mouth and
chewed noisily. She pushed bits of food around her plate.

"She's dead, killed herself."

"Oh." Madelyn sounded like she'd pricked her finger. "I
didn't know."

He touched her cheek. "Of course not."

He didn't say more then, but after the meal, we went to his
place and I sat with him in the kitchen while he made coffee.
Madelyn stayed in the living room, reading a magazine.

"What happened after Rivette left Paris?" I asked, perching
on a stool.

He took coffee beans from the fridge. "You want the whole
story?"

"Yes."

He rubbed his mouth, then filled a kettle with water and put
it on the stove. He poured beans into a grinder and held up a
finger while the machine churned raucously. When it stopped, he
said, "Nuns took her to a convent, but after the war she had no
money. She was alone, only fourteen."

"Same age as me."

He scanned my face. "Yes. I always imagine her more
grown-up, but she couldn't have been." He spooned the ground
coffee into an espresso pot. "She went to work for farmers. They
only wanted her to clean house and care for the animals. They
gave her rags to wear."

"Then what happened?"

He met my eyes. "She was raped. The father and three
sons."

I saw haystacks, a girl pushed down, her eyes open. The

hands on her were large, meaty, cold. She smelled animal waste, rotting feed, onions, and sweat.

"She would never say much about this time. When she was sixteen, an uncle found her and took her to Palestine. Later, she came to the States." He put the coffeepot on the stove. "She didn't write to us until she came here. I think she was ashamed. I think she felt like a failure for not saving her parents. I know it's absurd, a little girl against the Nazis, but people are not rational."

He sat beside me. "She wrote when she felt stronger, and I went when I got the letter. I was so happy. I took it as a sign of *my* rescue. I was stagnating. Europe seemed full of death. I didn't even write to say I was coming, just showed up at her door, and do you know what, she recognized me." His face fell. "She looked different, though, her eyes . . . pain."

He lifted the pot off the stove. "She liked the craziness of my arrival." He arranged a tray with cups, sugar, and lemon peel. "She was studying at Columbia, languages. I loved her as I always had, and we were happy. I worked at many jobs, but after a few months I met a man who owned a jewelry store on Madison Avenue. I met many rich women." He made a puffing sound. "They didn't tempt me. Rivette was full of fun, and many people loved her, but when she got drunk she'd say, 'Survival isn't all it's cracked up to be.' "

He put the coffeepot on the tray. "I should have believed her, but I thought we would get married and have children. I thought that's what she wanted, but one day when I came home I found her dead. Sleeping pills." He sat again. "Everything I had believed seemed a lie. The day had seemed ordinary, but it wasn't the day. She couldn't recover from the war. Maybe I will never recover from her."

"You will."

He roughed my hair. "Not every unhappiness has a solution."

I didn't believe him then.

⚡

I trusted his calm, though, the serenity he gathered around him. His apartment, on Broadway and Eighty-ninth Street, faced the back—cavelike, casual. A pale blue spread covered the bed and dust balls sat beneath chairs. Unframed posters were tacked on the walls. In the bathroom, James Dean straddled a motorcycle. In the kitchen, Charlie Parker grinned in a beret. In the hall, a Paris fountain gently spouted. The living room quartered a coffee table and a couch, but was otherwise given over to painting. Blank canvases leaned against a wall. Jars of pigment and tubes of paint lined another, and a large easel commanded the center. The industry and dreaminess sparked a memory.

In Washington Heights, at a certain point each afternoon, the big kids would split off from the younger ones. "You can't come," Madelyn would say, as I begged to follow her to the grass beside the Catholic church or join the game of statues getting under way. My heart would sink as she trailed off, and sometimes I'd sulk until she returned. At other times, I'd play potsy with the lot left behind, feeling us a scraggly band of rejects. At yet other times, I'd wander by myself or with some kids to the cigar factory that flanked the candy store.

The cigar factory was really a small shop, where workers, with skin brown and wrinkled as tobacco, twirled leaves into cigars. They would gesture for us to enter and speak to us in Spanish, a few words of which I understood. The place smelled of beer and spicy stew, which simmered in a blackened pot. Stacking the cigars, the men would sing cascading melodies, and sitting cross-legged on the wooden floor, I'd stare at the perfectly formed cylinders, mounting in pyramid stacks, and forget everything but the moment. At five, when my sister would come, I'd sometimes wish she'd go away.

Jacques was the first person I knew who felt aloneness as a pleasure. "It's the most wonderful feeling," he'd say. "I listen to jazz, and my insides become still. I work, and when I look up hours have passed." His paintings were less satisfying. The canvases were everywhere, all portraits of women with gold skin, slender jaws, bright robes, and dead eyes. They seemed stuck, murky. It wasn't possible to tell what he wished to convey.

Still, his industry inspired me. I confessed my interest in art, and he composed a still life–a wine bottle, an apple, a pear, and a loaf of bread. He showed me how to sharpen charcoal, lay on a color field, and bring up light. One day, to further my education, he took Madelyn and me to the Museum of Modern Art.

"This is my favorite place in New York," he said, passing through the doors. "Well, there are many favorite places, but when I come here I feel serious. Not too much, so I am afraid to work. It's a delicate balance, no?"

Madelyn nodded, amused. Jacques slipped his arm around her waist, moving slowly, measuring their power to attract. Jacques led us to Degas, Manet, Monet, and Bonnard. He studied a Matisse, a figure seated at a piano before an open window. "It is fantastic the daring, almost abstract, letting a little say so much." At a Braque, he said, "Look at the sense of design."

I saw planes and shifts of tone, some creating openness, others closure. "It looks like the sidewalk after a rain."

"Good," he said.

We worked our way to more contemporary painters. When we arrived at Balthus, my heart sped. Girls with slim bodies and mysterious faces were exposing themselves before men or were being spied on, and the females exulted in the attention. Balthus was obsessed with certain shapes and moods, but here was an artist diving into his obsession in order to retrieve a general truth.

A painting of an angry man and a seated girl was particularly arresting. The paunchy man wore a striped bathrobe. He stared out defiantly, but there was anxiety around his mouth, as if he were watching something shocking outside the frame of the painting. Behind him sat the girl. Light brown hair waved about her face, and firm breasts peeked from her camisole—one breast was almost fully exposed. She was in the background, bathed in fleshy light. She wasn't looking at the man, but it was clear she'd set his panic in motion.

"The girls remind me of me," Madelyn said.

Jacques brushed her cheek with the back of his hand and held her chin, moving her face from side to side. "You were never so coy."

"You're wrong. I did pretend to be innocent. I wish I'd been as flagrant as them."

Jacques appealed to me.

"I'm with her."

"No! Balthus is a pasha. The sex is cloying, like duck sauce."

"Umm," Madelyn said.

He swatted her, and she darted away. She let him catch her, and they laughed, their bodies touching. They talked softly, and I caught something about a restaurant, but soon I stopped listening and their voices became a hum.

I floated to the ceiling, noting people gazing at the paintings, some awed, others fidgety. No one noticed me, except the girl in the painting, who beckoned. I lowered my legs, until I was standing in midair, and walked into the painting. As I approached the girl, she turned, her hair fanning, her gray eyes steady.

"Why do you stay on that chair?" I asked.

She stood, stretching her arms. She adjusted the camisole so that it covered her breasts. "It's nice to see I *can* rise." She pointed to the chair. "Want a turn?"

I sat, noticing how beautiful my skin looked in the light. I smelled the sharp, clean scent—like cloves—she'd left. And then I felt a sucking force and my skin began to tingle. "What's that?"

"The artist's eyes. How do you feel?"

"Hungry."

"It goes away, then you think about how lovely and young you are."

"That's all there is to do?"

She drew up her neck. "It's better to be at the service of art than cut up fruit." She looked at her fingernails. "At least that's what they say."

"Is the artist nice?"

She circled me. "No. He doesn't think I'm real." She looked at me beseechingly. "You think so, don't you?"

"You're the realest thing in the world. I've always thought so." The room was spacious, comfortable. A large sofa sat in the center; a patterned rug covered the floor, but it had to be dreary to stay here all the time. "Don't you want to get out?"

She pointed into the distance. "See that frame? There's no way out."

"You sound so accommodating."

She crossed her arms. "Every situation has its limitations. Unfortunately the Robe hasn't learned that yet."

"What's his story?"

"The artist doesn't give us much history. He wants feeling from the gut."

"Does the Robe touch you?"

Her eyes narrowed. "No. Well, usually not. I think the artist and he are friends. Ask him yourself."

"He scares me."

She smiled. "He's just paint."

I went to him, and she resumed her place. The Robe was so engrossed in his thoughts, he didn't notice me until I stood directly before him. I asked, "What did she do to you?"

At first he tried to look through me, but when he realized I wasn't transparent he spoke. "What makes you think she did anything, *could* do anything? She's a stand-in for another girl."

"*She* thinks she real."

"I imagined her that way."

"She seems real to me."

"I have a vivid imagination."

"Where is the original girl?"

"Oh, it's a sad story. We were mountain climbing. She went to the aid of a struggling man. He was rescued, but she fell to her death." His eyes clouded with tears. "It should have been me."

I patted his shoulder. "It was just bad luck."

"Now I have *her* to remind me of my loss. She is my shame."

"Is that why you're so angry?"

"Am I?"

"You should see your face."

"There aren't any mirrors."

I stood on my toes. "Look in my eyes."

He leaned close, and I inhaled a rooty smell. He peered and flinched. "*I'm a prisoner of memory,* a shadow in the artist's fancies."

"How terrible."

"You needn't look superior."

"Was I?"

"You don't know your own feelings any more than me. Do you imagine you are any less a shadow to others? Do you think they aren't interchangeable shadows to you?"

"Is there no escape?"

He shrugged. "Dreaming, and maybe painting."

"That's what I'll do."

He put his hands on his hips. "Well, you can't fall into art the way you traipsed into this painting. If you want to pose sit in a chair. If you want to paint pick up a brush."

He grimaced, and I leapt back, losing my footing. When I regained my balance I was in a limbo place, with vapor all around. There was a brush in my hand and beside me tubes of paint. I could still see the figures. The girl's face was shaped like a teardrop. The blue in the carpet was sapphire—darker than the azure in the window. I squeezed Paine's gray onto a palette and painted a piano. The girl went to it. The Robe turned, and I painted his arms so they reached out—but whether to embrace or ensnare her I didn't know. In a smoky voice she sang "Ain't Nobody's Business but My Own." At first the Robe resisted the rhythm, but in time his body began to sway and his face softened, becoming a smudge. Then all I saw was my hand painting.

I began to doubt Serge after I met Jacques. Jacques, the bohemian loner, seemed the antithesis of my social, brainy analyst. I enthused about Jacques to Serge, relaying the tale of Rivette. For a while Serge just listened, but my enthusiasm mounted, and one day he rumbled, "What is so appealing about this man? You do not make it clear."

"He's honest."

Serge bit into something hard. A carrot? "How do you know?"

"I sense it."

"Perhaps he is a good actor."

"Have you met him?"

"What do you think?"

"That you don't like him."

"Why?" He sounded surprised.

"Because you doubt me."

"I am trying to discover the basis for your feelings." He let out a small sigh. "What else interests you about him?"

"He's an artist. I want to be one too."

"What else?"

"Don't you care that I want to paint?"

"What do you think?"

"No."

"Why?"

"Because you didn't say anything encouraging when I told you."

"What would you like me to say?"

" 'It's great.' "

"It's great. Are you satisfied?"

"No."

"Why?"

"I want you to say more."

"What?"

"That you like artists, that you can imagine me as one."

"I can only help you see yourself, whatever materializes. Besides, I don't know what an artist looks like."

"What do you think I should be, then?"

"Aware of your desires."

"What *else?*"

"That's all I can want for you."

I sighed.

"Why the sigh?"

"I want you to have ambitions for me."

"But that is the opposite of being an artist, no? An artist determines his own course. Think about it." He bit into a stick of celery, and I felt I was being crunched. According to Serge, wanting his approval meant I wasn't destined to paint. "Can we get back to Jacques?" he asked.

"Fine."

"What else comes to mind? Shut your eyes."

"Rivette."

"Yes?"

"I don't know anymore."

"Think."

I saw haystacks. "She's on the farm."

"Yes?"

"There's a man in overalls with an ugly face. His suspenders are down."

"What happens?"

"He's gets on top of her."

"What does she do?"

"Nothing. She thinks she'll die if she fights. She thinks she'll die no matter what she does."

"Why do you imagine total disaster when Rivette survived?"

"I always make things worse than they are. You know me."

"Not as well as you would like to believe, but I will tell you what I think."

I gripped the couch.

"You identify with this girl, because Jacques loved her, and you wish to attract him too."

"I know."

"But perhaps you don't know everything. You want him because he belongs to your sister. You feel guilty and you think some terrible punishment will befall you, like rape. You think you deserve it, and maybe a part of you wants it for that reason."

"I *like* Jacques. I'd like him even if he weren't Madelyn's. *You* don't like him, because Madelyn and I do. I thought about Rivette to please you. *You* make me feel I have to give in."

"When I show you what you do not wish to see, then I am a torturer. Otherwise, I am your friend." His voice was steady, warm. "I am not telling you whom to like. I am saying *you* fear you will be punished if you want your sister's man."

I didn't want to struggle. I let his certainty surround me.

⚜

But other doubts arose. In the middle of another session, he asked why I twirled my hair.

I shrugged. "I always do."

"You want me to know you masturbate."

I dropped the hair. "I don't. I don't even know how."

"You are signaling me from your subconscious that you are a sexual being. You don't need to be ashamed." His voice was soft. Flirtatious? "I don't think there is anything wrong."

When I got up from the couch and saw him smiling, I felt like I was masturbating right in front of him.

The next week, he showed me sexual paraphernalia. Out of his desk came a condom and a diaphragm. He pinched the diaphragm to illustrate its flexibility. Off a shelf came an anatomy book, and side by side we examined genitalia. I saw long, thick, rosy, pale, limp, and erect penises. I saw penises in far greater detail than Jerry's, as well as baggy and tight scrota. I saw pubic hair, labia, clitorises, cervixes—and a prodigious number of hymens. Some were walled over. Some had little perforations. Some had larger holes, irregular and jagged, and some had one opening in the middle, the shape of a keyhole.

Serge kept wondering if I had questions. I was silent. I felt like my eyes were being scarred. I tried to pull inside myself, but he was there too.

"The hymens are quite different, no two exactly the same, like snowflakes."

All I could think about was how guttural his accent sounded and how old-fashioned he looked in his bulky brown jacket. He reminded me of my grandmother. I laughed.

"What's funny? The snowflakes?"

I laughed harder.

"What is funny?" He looked hurt, and I tried to stop, but I couldn't.

He ended the session early. The first time.

⚜

I was still laughing when I reached Madelyn's and grew even giddier when I learned Jacques was taking us to dinner.

This was not to prove one of my better days. Jacques had discovered a promising bistro, and the meal started out fine. He ordered snails, pâté de foie gras, coq au vin, and rack of lamb with rosemary. Madelyn and I thought everything wonderful, and Jacques, in general, was pleased too. For dessert there was crème brûlé and chocolate mousse, then espresso and the check. That's when the trouble began.

Adding it, Jacques's eyes winced the tiniest bit, and on the street, Madelyn took a twenty-dollar bill from her purse, whispering in my hair, "He doesn't need to pay for us." She handed him the money, but he waved it away. She said, "Oh, come on, I'd rather have you take it from me than some other women."

He went white. "Where does *your* money come from? Your father? I'm no more a whore than you."

Madelyn stayed cool. "I didn't say you were, darling. All I said is I'd rather you take the money from me. I'm trying to save myself grief. Is that so terrible?"

He made a puffing sound and raised his hands. We walked silently for a while, but when Madelyn shoved the money in his pocket, he didn't protest. He put his arm around my shoulder and said, "I'm sorry," but he didn't look romantic anymore.

At my next session, Serge, the wise counselor, was back, and I talked willingly about stealing men and besting females. At the end of the hour, he grinned and said, "This year you come to the barbecue."

Each fall, Serge held a cookout at his country house. My parents and sister had gone in the past, and now—joy—I was to be included too.

Saturday morning, we packed into my father's Oldsmobile and drove up the Hudson to Grotten, playing initials and twenty questions. After three hours, we turned onto a dirt road, continued for a mile, then came to a rustic, weathered house set amid towering pines. A slew of cars was parked outside, but no one answered when we knocked. My father pushed open the door. I felt light-headed stepping over the threshold.

But there was nothing strange on the other side. The room looked like Serge's office, only larger and more informal. On one side was a kitchen, on the other a combination dining room/living room. Threadbare oriental carpets lay on the floors. Ashes coated the fireplace. Blankets and afghans draped a couch and armchairs. And papers and books overran tables and a desk that faced a picture window.

A screen door banged, and Serge appeared, wearing a plaid shirt, moccasins, and a red cotton scarf. Even in this Yankee garb, he looked foreign; it was the way he wore scarves, casual yet elegant. "Welcome to my *dacha*." He spread his arms. My mother and sister hugged him. My father shook his hand, and I said "Hi."

"Come outside." He led us from the living room to a bedroom, where there was a desk, a dresser, and a brass bed. His bed. I imagined him waking up, blinking, unsure whether he was conscious or dreaming. This room led to a screened porch, filled with wicker furniture and luxuriant potted ferns. I saw Serge there with friends, sipping tea. The porch emptied onto the backyard, which disappeared into woods. The grass shone lustrously in the early fall sun. But the guests were the most marvelous aspect—holding tinkling glasses, talking, radiating pleasure, glamour.

"The fire is started. There is food and wine. Go, meet." Serge took my hand. "You, I show you my place."

We walked to a pine grove which opened onto a small pond. The sun was high, and everything looked golden. There were lilies on the water and a tangle of cattails at one end of the pond. A swan mother and three babies glided by.

"It's beautiful, ya?"

"Ya."

He rubbed his stomach. "Fifteen acres is mine. I was quite lucky to buy when I did. The values have skyrocketed in the last five years." This talk surprised me; my father always painted Serge above money.

The path led through wilder growth. "Still mine." It was cool amid the trees. Ferns glistened with moisture, and the sun, peeking through, dappled the earth. We reached another clearing, in which sat an elegant stone house with a pitched slate roof and two skylights. Surrounding it was an immaculate garden. "Lovely, no? It's Wildeweiss. You will meet him, my oldest friend in America."

I tried to imagine this man. He would be tall, like Serge, but fit. He'd have to have something over his friend to merit his confidence, and I couldn't imagine anyone smarter. Back at the party, Serge greeted new arrivals and I searched for Wildeweiss, electing a distinguished man with graying sideburns, wearing a blue blazer with gold buttons. "Who's that?" I asked Madelyn.

"Ames. He was on my trip. He's been seeing Serge the longest. Very rich."

"How'd he make his money?"

"Investments."

"Why does he see Serge?"

"His wife left. He's lonely."

"Can Serge fix that?"

She nodded. "Whatever's the matter."

Ames was talking to a woman who looked familiar. Then I remembered her; she had been at Serge's my first day. Ames looked eager to please. The woman exuded confidence. All the other women at the party wore dresses and looked fragile, leaning on furniture or men. They stood with their feet pointed out, and their arms wrapped around themselves. This woman wore tan slacks, a matching, belted sweater, a large silver bracelet, and dangly earrings. She stood squarely, pulling fingers through her hair.

She drifted from Ames and talked to a small, slim man with

intelligent eyes and a sly grin. He listened when she spoke,
clicking off points. He made her laugh, but their camaraderie was
free of flirting.

Serge slipped among the guests. With some he smiled, with
others he argued and teased. He was unchallenging with
Madelyn. With my parents, he broke into Yiddish, telling a story
with reversals of fortune. I couldn't hear all the words, but he
gestured broadly, opening his eyes wide. My parents stood with
their hands behind their backs, their faces tilted toward him.

"You'll have them eating out of your hands," Wolf whispered in my ear. I jumped. He kissed me, looking blindingly
handsome in a white linen suit. His elegance was almost out of
place amid the casualness of Serge's environment. Corinne was
by his side, dressed in a peach linen suit and matching sandals.
She was tan too, exactly the same shade as Wolf. They looked
like members of the same family, and I wondered if, in time,
everyone in Serge's circle came to look somewhat alike.

"How was your trip?" Corinne asked.

"Great."

"Get to Esalen?"

"Nuh uh."

"Too bad. It's wild, cliffs over the sea. I've never felt so
free." She cocked her head and glanced at Wolf. "Wait till Serge
takes you on a trip. He comes to a new place, and it's as if he's
always lived there. In Italy, you think he's Italian, in France, he
seems French. You fit right in too. You'll see."

"What will she see?" Bliss poked in. She was as thin as ever.
Her skin was stretched so tightly over her bones, it looked like it
might tear. Wolf moved off, and she trailed him with her eyes.

"I was telling Julie about traveling with Serge."

Bliss snorted.

"Don't be a snob."

"Yes, your majesty." She bowed to Corinne. "Love your
shoes. Bonwit's?"

"Galleries Lafayette. Apologize to Julie."

"Yeah," I said.

Bliss lowered her shoulders, and I noticed how skinny they were, like the littlest kids at camp who turned blue during a swim. "Everybody gets to travel with Serge. It's no big deal."

"You're impossible," Corinne said.

Bliss slipped her arm through her friend's. "But you love me anyway."

Corinne gave her a sidelong glance. "Don't be so sure."

"Well," Bliss said, looking contrite, "I guess I should get to work. Would you believe Serge has me typing today?" She feigned exasperation but looked so pleased her face was almost full. She bounded to the house.

"What's she talking about?"

"She types letters and articles for Serge, a part-time job. Didn't Madelyn tell you?"

I shook my head.

"Too busy with Jacques, I guess. Bliss types the work after Dr. Wildeweiss corrects the English." She pointed to the small, intelligent-looking man. "Bliss works for Serge, and I work for *her* father. Musical chairs. Madelyn's the only one working for her actual father, but you know Madelyn, she never pretends to be anyone."

"What do you do for Wolf?"

"Catalog prints. I'm learning tons, tons. Of course he doesn't take me seriously. They don't," she said, gesturing to the men.

"Why not?"

"I suppose it's because we let them. Serge probably sees Bliss's job as occupational therapy. Wolf is patting me on the head, the way your father patronizes Madelyn."

I pointed to the woman with salt-and-pepper hair. "What about her?"

"Tana? She's a professor. Men take her seriously, but I don't think they see her quite as a woman. Get the problem?"

She moved off, and I tried to grasp her meaning. On one

side were Tana and Dr. Prescott, women who were profitably occupied but lived without men. On the other side were Nadine and my mother, who wanted protection and wound up bullied or scattered. My mother and Nadine could rise up, surprising themselves, but they didn't count on their abilities. Madelyn, Bliss, and Corinne seemed headed in a similar direction, but they didn't appear motivated by fear. Corinne, especially, seemed aware of herself, characterizing her probable future not as the fulfillment of a dream but as a compliant stroll. What all the women had in common, though, was a sense of living out a script written by someone else.

I watched Tana. Whatever men thought of her, she didn't appear rocked. Serge was beside her, listening intently to what she said. When she ran a finger along her lower lip, he imitated the gesture. If he appreciated her, could he be like other men? He encouraged me to stand up to bullies, but was I supposed to think for myself around him?

Nadine was arranging flowers in a vase. When my mother approached her, she smiled indulgently. I joined them. My mother said to Nadine, "A woman of many talents. You are the *most* gorgeous thing."

"Oh, Thea, sugar, you look lovely too."

My mother jiggled her shoulders. "How do you like my Julie?" She tapped my arm. "Some of the baby fat's gone."

I'd given up Janet's lunches and lost a few pounds on my trip. I shot Nadine a "rescue-me" look, and she winked.

My mother dragged on her cigarette. "I told her it was a matter of control. I mean, we all want to eat. Right?"

"She looks adorable, Thee."

My mother tapped Nadine's shoulder and pointed at Serge, who was arranging meat on the grill. "Look at him with those horse steaks." Her smile faded. "That was my mother, always with the food."

Nadine watched him, and all irony slid from her expression. "He likes to take care." She looked at my mother with sincerity.

"Before I knew Serge, I thought things were absolute. I was taught that people were good or bad. Now I know they're pulled hither and thither by the past. But things can change."

My mother drifted off, but she snapped into focus when my father and Brett approached. My cousin was holding my father's hand. He kissed my mother. Nadine watched. Brett clutched him, then leaned toward me. "Charlie wants your sister."

I searched for Madelyn, and sure enough she was laughing with Corinne's brother, a man I'd met walking arm-in-arm with Bliss. He was a stockbroker, with blond hair and a sweet face. Madelyn was flashing her lashes and wrinkling her nose. "She's just being friendly," I said.

"You're simpleminded."

"I'm not."

"Everything is under your nose, but you don't see. Take Serge. You think he's God."

"I don't."

"I see the way you watch him. Well, let me tell you, feet of clay."

"What does that mean?"

She hit her forehead. "I keep trying to help you, but I can see you're going over the falls in a barrel."

She wandered off, and I wondered if Serge had shown her the sex books. She'd get over them. I had. She brushed past Wildeweiss, and I caught his eye. He smiled, a measured flit of the upper lip. We moved toward each other, meeting halfway. He held out his hand. "Felix Wildeweiss."

"Julie Stark. I know who you are."

"Who?"

"Serge's editor."

"Oh, I was hoping you'd surprise me."

"I will," I said, trying to sound sophisticated.

"Come with me." I followed him to a table with an umbrella. He took off his jacket, removed a wooden box from his breast pocket, and sat down, folding himself into the neatest possible package. The box contained a chess set, the pieces of which he lined up. "You may have white."

"I stink at this." Amy's brother had taught us the moves, but we'd preferred bombarding the pieces with marbles.

"It's just a game." He lifted an eyebrow.

"Okay." I dug into my memory for Judd's ploys, and after a few moves sacrificed two pawns and nipped Wildeweiss's defense.

"That's it. Take a chance!"

But I had nothing with which to back up the gambit, and he wiped me off the board in a dozen more moves. He wanted another game, and I played a little better the second time. He gave no leeway, however. He was out to win; any blood would do.

As he checkmated me for the second time, Tana perched on his chair. Her cheekbones looked chiseled. "Release that child."

"Do you see chains? Julie, Tana. Tana, Julie."

"Hello," we said.

"Your bonds elude the naked eye." Her accent was stronger than Jacques's but not as pronounced as Serge's. It had soft, hushing sounds, like leaves in wind. She leveled her gaze at me. "Do you know you are playing with one of the great mathematicians in this country?"

Wildeweiss waved at her impatiently. "Speaking of bondage, what is Columbia doing to you now?"

Tana squinched her mouth. "This year, I'm okay. After that, who knows? Not a new story."

"Tana teaches psychology at Columbia, where I am also employed."

Columbia triggered thoughts of Rivette, and I asked, "Did either of you know Rivette Vogel? She was a student."

Tana shook her head, but a light went on in Wildeweiss's eyes. "The name sounds familiar." He shook his head with frustration. "I don't have a picture."

"She studied languages. A friend of mine knew her."

"What languages?" Tana asked.

"I'm not sure. She was from France, but she spoke Polish originally."

Tana sat up. "I am Polish. What else do you know?"

"Not much. I was hoping you could tell me things."

"She's dead, isn't she?" Tana's mouth became a thin line. "How did you know?"

"I have a nose for extinction." She waved to us, " 'Bye," and moved off.

"I made her unhappy. I'm sorry."

"No. The war did and a thousand other things not even she knows. Listen, I think I did know this girl. Let me put my mind to it, I have tricks to jog the memory." He packed up the chess set and placed it in his pocket. "I will let you know the next time we meet."

So there would be a next time. Good. He joined Tana, who was smoking and leaning against a tree. But soon Serge called us to dinner, and we took seats around redwood tables, set end to end. My mother and sister sat together, giggling. Charlie and my father were across from them, my father calling Charlie "son," asking about the stock market. Charlie was like Woody, with his even features, blond hair, and tall, athletic build. Charlie kept his eyes on Madelyn, but she hardly noticed him. When she was with my mother, no one stood a chance.

Bliss sat next to Serge, waving away potatoes, bread, salad. Her eyes burned. Fleshless arms poked out of her chic dress, which, tiny as it was, stood away from her skeletal form. Her skin looked transparent, drained of color, as if she seldom saw light. Serge sliced two hunks of fat from a steak and carried them to the grill. He cooked them until they were charred and put them on her plate. She smiled through her lashes, and dimples showed in her thin cheeks. She cut a piece of fat, and chewed hungrily.

Serge shrugged. *"That* she will eat."

He was so gentle with her. A sweet smile suffused his thick features as he followed her fork from plate to mouth. He loved her, even though she seemed more an absence than a presence. Her need, her aloneness moved him, and I envied her that.

After the meal, people milled again. Wolf kept looking at Corinne, even when he was talking to someone else. His head moved back and forth, trying to locate her. She searched for him too, and I saw they were lovers. Was this the secret Brett said was under my nose? In the warm, sunlit air, it didn't seem dangerous. People changed partners. What had Corinne called it? Musical chairs.

Did Nadine know? She was beside Serge, stroking his arm. Serge was speaking in her ear, and she looked at him with naked trust. His eyes, too, saw nothing but her, and I realized that Nadine—not Bliss or Tana—was his favorite. Was it because she surrendered her judgments with the least reserve?

How did Serge keep everyone's secrets straight? It was his genius, that was it. He could digest whatever was real, any unhappiness or confusion. His energy was boundless; he chatted, carried drinks. He kept the circle from cracking. Everyone smiled and touched: hugs, kisses, arms slipped around waists, hair flicked off cheeks. We were a family—not a tribe huddled behind closed doors but a society of rich, generous Americans and serious Europeans, who linked us to the past.

There were no artists, I realized with a pang. I'd forgotten Jacques. But that was the trouble with Jacques. He was too separate, tenuous. He couldn't even compel Madelyn's loyalty.

I wanted to stay in the golden circle forever, with or without artists. But what would be my place? I didn't want to be where Bliss was, or Tana, or even Nadine. Maybe my place didn't yet exist.

Chapter 4

"IT'S GREAT HE'S asked you, it's really great." My mother made a clicking sound with her tongue.

A month had passed since the barbecue, and this week, at the end of my last session, Serge had said, "For the weekend, you come to my house?" "Yes," I'd answered. I was packing now, about to board the train for Grotten.

Tana was waiting at the station, wearing khaki slacks and a powder blue shirt made of old, soft material. She looked lighter in spirit than she had at the barbecue. Then I'd guessed her to be older than my mother, but now she looked younger. We hugged and packed into her red Corvette convertible. "You like?" she asked.

"I like."

"You didn't expect?"

"No."

"It's so American."

"So *fast*."

"Jazzy."

"Yeah."

"I'm not jazzy."

"Well, no."

She started the car, gunning the engine. "Well, yes. But that's the point." She zipped onto the road, flicking the shift like a joy stick. "I wanted something outrageous and expensive. We drive with top down?"

"Sure," I said, huddling in my jacket.

We speeded, and her cheeks grew red. "Orphans of the war want reparations."

"Tell me about the war."

"I was in medical school. Jewish students were not allowed to sit in classrooms. Ya, it's true. We had to stand. Eventually, we were not even allowed to go to school. My parents wanted me to leave Poland, especially my mother. She thought I was talented and should look somewhere else for opportunities. I didn't want to leave her, but when the situation grew desperate I went to France."

She hit the gas. "I was scared mouse, with only a few words of French. I am worrying about my family all the time, and with good reason. One day, after months, I walk into cafe, feeling very disconsolate. I order coffee, and a man speaks in Polish. 'You look as alone as me,' he says. I am startled, because the accent is Russian, yet his voice reminds me of home. Of course you can guess it was Serge. When he spoke, I could see ahead a little. He was already a psychoanalyst. I had no money for school, so I became something between his patient and student." She shot me a glance. "He saved my life, although I doubt he knew how bad I was, and so many people were worse. He may have known. I don't know what goes on in his head. I'm still too much his patient to probe."

Was I too little his patient, I wondered?

Tana pulled into a farm stand and we gathered apples, cider, and Indian corn. She held up an ear with blue and red kernels. "He will try to eat this."

Back in the car, she said, "Now for your story."

"I don't have one."

"Everyone does."

"Nothing's happened to me yet, nothing like the war."

"Then your story is good luck."

When we walked in, Serge was in the kitchen, by the stove, a wooden spoon dangling from his mouth. Spicy aromas filled the air. A platter of cheese, sausage, and pumpernickel sat on the counter. He jiggled the spoon like Groucho's cigar. Tana rested the groceries on a counter and kissed his cheek.

"Keep stirring." He gave her the spoon. "It must brown but not stick."

She shooed him off. He bowed to me. "Put your things in there." He pointed to a second bedroom. Tana's clothes were on one bed, so I put my bag on the other. In the living room, I gazed out the picture window. The sun was almost down, and the trees looked purple. "Beautiful," Serge said. "How's my stew?" He went to see, and I followed. "Veal with garlic, paprika, and sage. I could put in sour cream." He pulled a container from the refrigerator. "For my guests."

"They don't need it." Tana looked at me.

"I like it either way."

"What a diplomat." She shook her wrist.

"Sour cream isn't going to hurt anyone."

"He diets and goes to spas. He groans he's fat, and then he begs for sour cream." She popped a piece of sausage in her mouth.

He watched her chew, lifting the lid off the sour cream, sticking in a finger, and licking a glob of cream. He put the container on the counter and shut it but, a second later, spooned half its contents into the pot. With an air of absentmindedness, he ate another spoonful of cream. He tasted his concoction. He licked his lips, ate more cream, and dumped the remainder of the container into the stew.

He chose a bottle of wine from a rack and searched for an

opener. Tana tossed it to him, and as the metal glinted in the light, I guessed that the diaphragm in Serge's drawer belonged to her.

There was a soft knock and Wildeweiss entered.

"Hello, Felix," Tana said, gathering plates and silverware.

He rushed me to the couch. "I met Jacques."

Serge coughed.

I'd hardly seen Jacques since the barbecue.

"We were in an art gallery, the only two people. How could I not notice such a good-looking man? We arrived at the same painting, one of those Picasso Amazons. She was exuberant, running along a beach. 'I don't know why I like her,' I said, and he responded, 'She knows what she wants.' "

Tana brought hors d'oeuvres and sat down.

"We went for coffee, and he said he was a painter. I asked why he'd come to this country, and he mentioned Rivette. I knew at once she was your girl. It was so strange." He picked up a piece of cheese. "I did know her, it turns out. I counsel foreign students, and she came to several meetings. She was vivacious, and I remember thinking, 'This one will make out fine.' " He shook his head.

"It is amazing, this coincidence," Tana said. "It must have some meaning."

"I almost think it does."

"Faithless one." She turned to me. "I lived through the crazy war and still believe there are explanations for uncanny events. Felix, who has never seen any real danger, says there is only chaos, that everything is random and unpredictable. Does that make sense?"

"You prove my point."

Serge laughed.

"You're too clever for your own good."

"I believe in the patterns in nature."

"People are in nature."

"Oh, I know about the compulsions and repetitions you deal in, but you were talking about fate."

"You will see. There's a reason you met this man."

"Are you going to see him again?" I asked.

"We exchanged numbers. I hope so."

Serge carried the stew to the table and ladled out portions with hungry eyes. I took a bite, tasting a delicious whirl of flavors.

"*Jules et Jim* is marvelous, ya, ya. This Truffaut is smart on the pent-up energy of women," Serge said.

"But he's so romantic," Tana objected. "The woman is the only one with will, and she's destructive. I think Truffaut is infatuated by this, and I don't like, don't trust."

"Ach. Every man is infatuated by the destructive power of women. They think women can squash them, because their mothers were powerful. And every woman is mistrustful of this curiosity in men."

"Men mistake their fears for reality and call this the world. Women are right to be mistrustful."

Serge laughed and stroked her hand. "You don't need to be mistrustful of me." She didn't move her hand. He laughed again, still stroking her. "*Catch-22*, now that is contrived, no feeling." He squinched his face, as if the failure in the book hurt him.

"The emotion is purposely flat," Tana came back. "That is what war does to the insides."

He let her have the last word, enjoying her readiness to argue. He ate salad with his fingers. "I wrote to Kennedy. Felix edited it. I said, 'Don't be fooled by Khrushchev's act, this man is not a crude or stupid barbarian.' "

"Americans are so beguiled by surfaces," Tana said. Wildeweiss twittered his mustache. Tana said she was sickened by the Berlin Wall, and thoughts of Germany kindled memories of Bertolt Brecht, whom she'd met in California. "Very charming, very drunk. He shot a pistol in a bar, then cut his hand on glass." She shrugged. "Recklessness costs."

They went on, Serge asserting, Tana refuting and embel-
lishing, Wildeweiss catalyzing them as audience. Occasionally
they'd break into other languages, then translate for me.

After dinner, Wildeweiss went home and Serge made a fire.
I'd brought *Lord Jim* but didn't feel like plunging in. I browsed
through Serge's bookcases. "Take anything you want," he called.
The shelves were stuffed with classics and psychology books,
but a paperback on his desk, *The Spider's Nest*, caught my eye.
The cover showed a woman's tragic face against a red background, and across the top was written, "From the depths of
degradation, all the way to true fulfillment, one woman's shocking confession can finally be revealed."

"Read it," he called, seeming like a spider himself, aware of
my every move. I opened it. The heroine's name was Charlotte,
and she was seeing a psychoanalyst. So this was the hook–some
sort of research. The style was breathless, racy, and I wanted to
continue, but my eyes grew heavy. I said, "Good night," got
undressed, slipped under the covers, and slept dreamlessly.

◊

A note was by my bed when I awoke: "Gone to town. Be
back soon. Love, Serge and Tana." I put on a pale blue sweater
which my mother had bought me, camel slacks from my father,
and Nadine's silk scarf. I ate a bagel and carried my book outside.
It was one of those rare November days that feels like spring and
fills the chest with hope. At the pond, the cattails were ripe and
chocolate brown. The baby swans, almost as big as their mother,
took forays off, bobbing for insects, but kept returning to the
fold.

I sat on a bed of pine needles and opened the book.

Charlotte was beautiful, a blonde with almond-shaped
green eyes. She worked as a buyer of belts and handbags in a

fancy department store and had been unhappy for a long time. After several sessions with her analyst, she described a fantasy: A handsome man takes care of her, alternately petting and punishing her. She never knows which she is going to get. Sometimes, he starts with a spanking, sometimes lovemaking. But no matter what he does, he remains focused on her, and her thoughts are entirely absorbed by him.

Her analyst explained that she didn't have vaginal orgasms, only inadequate clitoral ones. In order to be a real woman, she would have to experience the proper kind. He advised her to get the fantasy out of her head and bought her a magazine catering to her "perversion," as he put it. At home, poring over the personal ads, she was excited and confused, but one ad arrested her: "Expert chef happy to whip difficult menus into shape."

She dialed the number, her palms cold and wet. She wished to please her analyst, and she was eager for the impending liaison. A man answered, and her heart leapt into her mouth. She made an appointment for two days hence, very businesslike, noting that the man's voice was surprisingly soft. Nonetheless, she was flooded with fantasies. She imagined her lover fair-haired, with flashing black eyes. She stopped eating and kept to herself. It was all she could do to get to work.

On the appointed evening, she rang the bell. She heard movement, and her knees buckled. The door opened, and before her stood a small man with close-cropped dark hair and rabbity teeth. Her heart sank, but she urged herself not to judge too soon. The man did not greet her but commanded her to follow. She did, trying to conjure a sexy mood, but she was repelled by the stark, motel furniture in his living room.

"Get undressed," he barked. She stared, and he gave the order again. This time she obliged, feeling embarrassed as she slipped out of her tailored suit.

"Sit," he commanded, and she lowered herself onto the couch, which was covered with rough wool and scratched her bare behind. In a moment, he was beside her, and to her amazement she felt charged. He did not touch her immediately but reached under the couch and withdrew a black leather bag. He opened it, extracting a leather riding crop. She felt herself becoming wet.

Without further ado, he pulled her across his lap and struck her backside with the crop. His strength surprised her, but there was no thrill. She felt mortified, and the crop stung. In her reveries, the beatings had never hurt. Now she winced as the crop came down again and again, speeding up. She could hear his breathing get faster too, and finally he let out a high "yip," which she took for his climax. The beating stopped and he righted her, saying, "Get dressed." That was it. Her behind felt sore as she slipped on her clothes, but the pain wasn't as keen as her frustration.

I put down the book, feeling as let down as Charlotte. Getting her wish had turned into a farce, but the fantasies had excited me. And confused me. I'd hated my father's spankings and felt no pleasure when Serge said I wished to be punished. But in Charlotte's reveries, when she'd thrilled to her lover's wild need and exulted in surrendering, the words had been electric.

It was noon when I returned to the house. Serge was alone. "You were walking?"

I nodded.

"Tana is with the horses. We have lunch?"

"Sure."

He pulled leftovers out of the fridge, and we nibbled from platters and pots. He reported on the morning's rounds: a trip to the post office, shopping for food, a drive to the stables. He ate sausage, bread, stew, cheese, fruit. He looked exhausted and sad, gravity tugging on his features. I wanted to give him something, but I could not think of anything he'd want. He brought a coffee cake to the table and chipped away at it with a knife, eating until only a sliver remained. He looked at it, surprised. He kept staring at it, and the silence was eerie. I began gathering the plates, and he flashed a smile so warm it made him look refreshed. "You are a good girl. Leave the plates for later. Come."

He led me to his room. I thought he was going to show me a photograph or a letter, something from the past, maybe from the war. But he didn't go to his desk. He sat on his bed, and with two swift motions kicked off his shoes. He leaned back and stretched, then patted the place beside him. It was a small gesture, the flick of a wrist.

My heart sped. I felt excitement and fear, the fear stoking excitement. It didn't seem possible to say no. I wanted to see how far he would go, and the awfulness made me giddy. I sat beside him and nothing happened. For a moment I thought I'd dreamed up the danger. Then he stretched voluptuously, his head searching for a pillow, his hand reaching for me, pulling me down, down.

He held me close. I inched to the edge of the bed like a thief and looked at the wallpaper. Roses swam across it. This had been a girl's room; a girl had conjured wolves here and awakened to purple light. Serge's breathing sounded like a storm, and then the air moved near me, and he reached under my sweater. He untied my scarf, drawing it over my skin. It felt like a knife. He gave each breast a squeeze. "They're fine. Your mother said you were worried they were too small."

I crawled into the word "small"—"schmall" he pronounced it. He stroked my stomach and thighs, and what he touched separated off. I smelled sausage and cigar. My skin tingled, like pinpricks. A part of me got off the bed, stood against the wall, and noted, "How interesting, he's massaging her neck, kissing her ear, running his hands along her behind." This part waded in the pond. The water was warm.

I don't know how much time elapsed before Serge sat up and looked at his watch. "We must stop," he said, as if ending a session. He swung his legs over the bed and slipped on his shoes. He smoothed his hair. "You're good."

I touched my arms. Still intact. I pulled down my sweater,

feeling Serge's hands. My body wasn't mine anymore. I'd never liked it, but I still had to lug it around. How long? I picked up *The Spider's Nest* and went back to the woods. I must have walked for an hour before coming to a clearing. I cried sitting against a tree, then stopped, looking at my feet. My Pappagallos looked so innocent. They didn't belong on me anymore.

Sun streaked through the leaves, dappling the earth. Bark and branches cast shadows: darks, lights, and medium tones. There were larger shapes next to my legs. The patterns were intricate, expanding as far as I could see, and I kept seeing: squirrel holes, anthills, grass spiking from the ground, a tender shade of green.

I read.

Charlotte kept fantasizing, and her analyst told her to return to the Riding Crop. She didn't want to, but she complied. The second time, the Crop proved just as methodical and aloof, and she began to despair. Finally her analyst laid out her problem.

Charlotte's mother, who had died when Charlotte was nine, had been a cold, haughty woman. An expert horseback rider and a great flirt, she had spun in and out of Charlotte's life, taking myriad lovers. In Charlotte's fantasies, the men who alternately loved and punished her stood for her mother. Charlotte had lesbian tendencies. The proof was that she liked to masturbate and couldn't fully give herself to men. She was angry at males for stealing her mother and felt guilty about the rage. That's why she craved punishment. The beatings gave her the freedom to go on envying as well as to continue hating. But there was hope for her: Her failure to enjoy the beatings proved she was ready to change. All she had to do was admit that competing with men was hopeless. Then she could get everything she wanted.

At first Charlotte was mortified by this explanation, but in time she saw she did envy men, not only her mother's lovers but her younger brother as well; when he was born it had seemed the sun was setting on her happiness. Once she owned up to her jealousy, she envied men all the time. But her analyst insisted that men and women must have different fates. She cried listening to this, and as the tears flowed, she became aroused. It felt good, and she didn't want to stop. She thought it might be a sign of her masochism, but her analyst assured her it was mental health.

A few months later, she met a dentist she didn't envy, and the analyst said she could look forward to orgasms in her vagina. At the end of the story, she was waiting expectantly.

I closed the book, a sour taste filling my mouth. Did Serge think I was like Charlotte? Was he supposed to cure me?

Back at the house, Tana was lighting a fire. "We thought we'd lost you. We'll go horseback riding tomorrow?"

"Sure." I stood close to her, noticing how slim she was. Serge's door was closed. Good.

"Wolf and Nadine are fighting. They arrive soon. They always get quiet here."

Wolf was coming! That was wonderful. Everything would be all right. "Do you need help with the fire?"

She shook her head. "We don't need to worry about food. They bring lots. Part of ritual." She plumped pillows and stacked the magazines. I stayed close.

A car pulled up and a horn beeped. "Hello," Wolf boomed through the stillness. "We're here, we're here."

They entered, laden with shopping bags, Nadine in white fur, Wolf in a navy coat and matching hat. He was tan—he was always tan—and his pearl scarf emphasized the darkness. They put down their bags and spread their arms. I moved toward Wolf, Tana toward Nadine. Then Nadine hugged me—hugged the sweater Serge had pawed. "Hmm—I need a girl." Her powdered skin looked like a moth's wing. I was afraid to touch her.

Serge came out, his smile embracing everyone. Nadine went to him. "So, children, what did you bring?" His eyes were wide.

Wolf unpacked the bags. "Lox, bagels, roast beef, turkey,

hard salami, and in here, in here, caviar, umm, let's have some, and these." He unpacked two bottles of champagne. "And this." He smiled wickedly, producing a lemon tart. He rubbed his hands together. "Tonight we feast. Hey, Julie?" He kissed my hair. "Oh, honey." I squirmed away and helped Tana arrange plates. Wolf opened a bottle of champagne. "Glasses, everyone get glasses." Tana handed them out, and Wolf poured.

Tana minced onions, toasted thin slices of bread, buttered them, and arranged them in a circle around a platter. In the center went the caviar.

Nadine was on the couch, Serge beside her, his arm along her shoulder, his voice consoling.

"The track," Nadine said.

Wolf slammed his fist on the counter.

I jumped. Tana said, "It's nothing."

Wolf banged a cupboard door, making the dishes rattle, then went to Nadine. "I love you, but what do you want?" His hands sliced the air.

She straightened her neck. "Honey, to be consulted." Serge looked at her adoringly.

"What don't I consult you?"

"You go, you spend money like water. It's all you."

"I *spend?* I make money to spend. I spend on you. What else is it for?"

"You spend so *you* feel good, but it's never enough."

"So what?" He sat. Serge moved to a chair.

"You disappear." Her hands were fists in her lap. "The kids ask where you are. I lie. You drop ten thousand at a poker game. You laugh. You say you're sorry, but a few days later you're wound up again. You scare me."

He put his hands over his ears. "Don't say that."

"Why not?"

"I'm *not* scary," he whined. He touched her arm. "I'll change." He stroked her, and her cheeks colored. She turned to Serge. "He does this all the time. What should I do?"

Serge shrugged.

She looked at Wolf, then at the ceiling, her eyes weary. I stared, willing her to end the violence. My uncle attended her every move, and she exulted in his attention. She didn't want to relinquish her power, but it had no form except refusing him. Finally, she slathered a toast point with caviar and held it to his lips. "I don't want you to starve."

He took a bite and chewed. He licked her fingers, and she smiled. He pretended to gobble her hand, getting black bits on her skin and around his mouth.

I moved to the window, and Serge joined Tana. He lifted slices of lox with his fingers and dangled them into his mouth, eating fast, barely chewing. Wolf kissed Nadine's neck, his skin glowing. She leaned her head against the pillows and made contented sounds. In a while, they grew bubbly, sipping champagne, and their excitement made the room vibrate. Serge and Tana went to them, and everyone took turns bringing food to Nadine, circling her. She looked wounded but peaceful. She only picked at her food but drank champagne steadily, her laughter getting silvery.

Wolf told a story about an auction. He'd bid too high and had to sell his car to pay the bill. "Would you believe I sold it to the man I outbid?" Another time, he bought a muddy canvas and discovered a Cézanne underneath. He lifted his glass to the air. "Worth half a million."

Serge called Wolf a monster and brushed hair off Nadine's cheek. Tana laughed at their stories. She didn't mention politics.

Serge didn't love my family. My mother ate with her mouth open. My grandmother had smelly feet. My father paid him money, but we were low. That's why he touched me.

At eleven, Serge yawned and in a drowsy voice announced where we would sleep. "Nadine goes with Tana, Wolf on the couch." He paused, seeming to count the places. In a tone of self-sacrifice he said, "Julie comes with me. I'll take the cushions off the porch couch and sleep on them. She can have the bed."

Time became liquid as I searched the faces. No one objected. No one said, "Wouldn't it be easier if Wolf and Nadine shared Serge's bed, Julie slept with Tana, and Serge took the living room couch?" No one asked why, if Serge was planning to make a bed with couch cushions, he and I needed to be behind his closed door. They must have wondered. Perhaps they dismissed the suspicion as a sign of their own perversity. He had taught them well about projecting dark fantasies.

Wolf blinked, as if drunkenness were making him see things.

I looked beseechingly at Tana. Her left eyebrow flickered. A sign of doubt? Jealousy? Her lips went tight, but she didn't speak. She might have reasoned that it wouldn't help me and would only sever her from Serge. Perhaps she didn't believe what was about to take place. There was always a point where Serge could get her to back off.

I looked at Serge, willing him to change his mind, but his eyes darted. He yawned, though he looked lively. His cheeks were flushed.

I turned to Nadine, but she slipped her arm around my shoulder and said, "Lucky you. Brett never feels peaceful until Serge tucks her in."

I looked for doubt in her, but it wasn't there. Perhaps she couldn't imagine Serge wanting anyone but her. Was this what Brett had meant by "feet of clay"?

I didn't protest. I felt locked in the secret with Serge, and all I could do was cling to the hope that he really would make up a separate bed. Maybe the afternoon had been a test. Maybe I'd passed.

I went to the room, undressed, and put on my nightgown. It was flannel, with lace on the collar and cuffs, one of my mother's hated purchases, but now I huddled in it. I tried to hang onto tomorrow. I'd be in my own bed. But when Serge entered, wearing a striped bathrobe, the future vanished.

He didn't speak but slid under the covers and moved close. I could feel arousal in his warm breath beating at the back of my neck and in his fingers, which quickly worked their way beneath my nightgown. He stroked my breasts so long, I thought it was all that he would do. His fingers fluttered across my arms and shoulders and slowly inched their way down my back, tickling, massaging, more expert than Madelyn's.

He made new, more authoritative moves. He teased my nipples, first one then the other, squeezing, plucking. Streaks of heat shot to my crotch. How amazing that he could touch one part of my body and cause another to shiver. There was a sensitive spot between my thumb and forefinger, and when I rubbed it something itched under my tongue, but I'd never known there were other corridors of sensation. He stroked my hips, then moved beneath my underpants. Slowly, he rubbed his hand along the crease in my ass, spreading my cheeks, burrowing toward my crotch, seizing, exploring.

Fingers pushed into my vagina. Where were they going? The pictures weren't a help. Fingers flickered higher up, sending sparks to my breasts, my throat. Serge turned me, so we were face-to-face. His lashes fluttered near his cheeks. His lips were moist, parted, his features melting. "Touch me," he said. I didn't move. His robe was open, and underneath he wore trunks. He took my hand and placed it on a bulge. Something jumped, like mice under a handkerchief, and he murmured, "Miriam."

I pulled my hand back. His fingers probed me again, deeper. I bit my lip. He put his arms around me, pulling me closer, his chest touching mine. I smelled corned beef and champagne. His odor filled me. He took his penis out and inched his hips against mine. I wiggled back, but his hands were in me, pinning me. He kept working, waiting. I heard a moan. It was mine. He worked me faster, and it felt good, floating past land and civilization.

I rode his hands and felt his penis on my leg, a fist against a door.

"Darling," he whispered, drawing his body over mine. "Miriam," he said, and I felt a cold wave.

I opened my eyes. He seemed far away. I pushed against his arms. "Stop."

He looked at me. "All little girls want to sleep with their daddies."

"You're not my father, and I'm not Miriam."

"What?" He rolled off me.

"You called me 'Miriam.' "

He winced.

"Who is Miriam?" I sat up, smoothing my nightgown and watching his face freeze. I laughed. "Miriam, Miriam."

He pulled his robe closed.

"Miriam."

He swung his feet over the side of the bed.

"Miriam."

He held up his hands.

"Miriam, Miriam, Miriam," I hissed, and he fled to the porch.

I rolled to the center of the bed, stretching my arms and legs triumphantly, but the pleasure didn't last. I felt cold and clutched the covers. I burrowed down, pulling the blankets around me, but no matter how I turned I couldn't get warm.

In the morning, the first thing I saw was Serge's crumpled face. He was at his desk, in his robe, his shoulders slumped forward, his hair uncombed. The moment felt intimate, and I wondered where he'd spent the night.

Tana and Nadine were in the kitchen, drinking coffee. "Hi, dear," Tana said. My aunt smiled. She was wearing a rose dressing gown that matched her fingernails. The women shot looks at Serge, like nervous wives. Had he gone to one of them? Both?

"Good morning," I said.

Serge jerked his chin, a tiny gesture filled with distaste. I got dressed and packed up my things. In the bathroom, I looked at my helmet of hair, my soft face. I no longer believed I'd ever have cheekbones. When I went out, Wolf, Nadine, and Wildeweiss were at the table, Wolf high, his voice booming, his skin taut and ruddy. Tana laid out bagels and lox and poured coffee. Serge presided charmingly. Wildeweiss watched. I didn't eat.

"Let's walk," Wildeweiss said after the meal. The air was crisp; the sultriness had disappeared. We followed a trail of trees, marked with stripes of yellow paint. I wanted to tell him what had happened, for it seemed until I did I would never be able to say what I meant again.

"I met Serge when he stepped off the boat from Casablanca," Wildeweiss said. "I was there to meet him, at the dock. I worked with a group that was rescuing Jews. Serge had a reputation, but still it was hard to get him out. We pushed and wrote letters and finally brought him here in 1940.

"You should have seen him, a dark head of hair and thin as a bean pole. Yes, the fat is only since America." Wildeweiss pulled a pinecone from a tree. "Perfectly symmetrical. In nature there is order, but only there." He put the pinecone in his pocket. "Serge is the easiest man to know. He'll do anything for friends. He had five sisters. People from large families are often generous."

We came to a stream and crossed it, tiptoeing on rocks. "Look," he said, when we got to the other side. In the center of a clearing sat a huge boulder, twenty feet in diameter, looming gigantic amid ferns and small stones.

"How did it get here?"

"That's the magic question. Probably from a glacier, but there's nothing around nearly its size. It's a freak."

On one side was an emerald curtain of moss. Another area was flat, and on top grew a miniature forest, mostly shrubs and one large fir tree.

"The roots are cracking it," he observed.

The boulder was indeed fractured, split like a brain, and the roots were pushing into the crevice, burrowing to the rock's core.

"In time it will split in half," Wildeweiss whispered. "It's just a matter of time."

"How much?"

His mustache flickered. "Maybe a hundred years. By then everything in mathematics will be different. Everything we now think won't matter at all."

I didn't believe in such a time.

We trekked back and Wildeweiss departed. When I walked in, Serge was at his desk, and I wanted to open up my heart—even then—but I had no words. He looked up. "They have gone to see antiques. Wolf has to know what everyone else has."

"I have to leave. Homework."

"Of course. Tana will drive you to the station. Soon they come back for lunch, and she will take you. Whatever you want."

When I went to get my things, he followed, and for a moment I thought he meant to start again. He sat on the bed, but he was wearing a new look. Caution? "Don't tell your mother. She wouldn't understand."

Did he think my father would "understand" any better? "Okay," I said, not knowing what else to say. It seemed we were striking a bargain, and I felt I was getting gypped. What did I want? To wipe out the past. Since that was impossible, there was nothing I wanted.

The others returned. "You're not leaving?" Wolf said.

"Got to, homework."

"Ahrr, honey, it was great seeing you, just great." He hugged me hard, and I felt his muscles. "You're gonna break hearts, kid. You're gonna break hearts."

"We'll go horseback riding next time," Tana said. I didn't look at her. I placed *The Spider's Nest* on Serge's desk.

"Did you like it?" Nadine asked.

"I kept wanting to know what would happen."

"That's good enough for me." She smiled.

At the door, Serge took my hand. "Goodbye."

"Goodbye," I said, and two hot tears plopped out of my eyes.

∿

In the train, I watched the passengers. An old man with sparse gray hair was asleep. His head was thrown back, and it bobbed, making him look pathetic. A girl my age sat beside her mother. They had the same carrot-colored hair, so intense it looked fake. And they wore it pulled back on either side with barrettes. They passed a Coke back and forth, not talking, gazing at the scenery, like sheep peering from a pen.

It didn't matter that the man would die soon, the girl and her mother stay the same. It didn't matter whether I became thin, or sat at the center of a glittering circle. It didn't matter that I would keep going to Windsor, wearing my Pappagallos, or that, when these shoes wore out, another pair would take their place. I'd just keep walking, wearing out shoes. I'd get up each morning, because my heart would keep beating. I'd eat, because my fingers would grab food. I'd paint the shapes leaves made on the forest floor, but painting wouldn't lead me to the future. There were only patterns, an endless, repeating array. I'd wonder how I was supposed to grow up, but it would only be an exercise, because now I knew there was no such thing.

Between

FOR A LONG time, I didn't tell my parents. Serge explained I wasn't ready for psychoanalysis. They didn't question him, and I went along.

I ate. I got so fat, no one would go out with me except Paul Thomas, a boy from Windsor who'd quit college and spent his days cruising around in his father's car. I was familiar with the symptom from Madelyn's return, and given my depression, it seemed I belonged with Paul. He took me to movies in the city, always with subtitles. He put his arm around me, but he didn't kiss me. I thought Serge had ruined me.

In the middle of my junior year, my parents moved back to the city. "It was like we needed permission from Serge," my father said. He sold our house to the first people who looked at it. "They don't have much money, but they love the place, Thee, all the things we did." He threw in everything from our suburban life: the barbecue, the patio furniture, the electric lawnmower, the golf clubs, my bike.

Serge also got credit for Madelyn's engagement to Charlie Burkhardt. "He asked you to marry him?" My mother's cheeks were flushed. "I can't believe it. Yes, I can. What? My kid should go with a poor foreigner?" Madelyn had confessed her affair with Jacques, just at the time she dumped him, thereby saving herself grief and giving my parents something to cheer. "There were rocky days, but knock wood." My mother rapped her knuckles on Stuart's coffee table. "We came through, thanks to Serge."

I didn't think Serge had fixed Madelyn. He certainly hadn't fixed my mother. After the move, she was as restless as before. And disappointed that Nadine seldom called. She dove into decorating, discarding Stuart's pieces, applying most of her energy to my room. A table was delivered. Glass-topped, with wrought-iron leaves and spindly legs, it was meant to suggest that a feminine, willowy person used it. Then came a pink bureau with gold trim. And one day, when I came home—I commuted to Windsor by train—I found two paintings over my bed.

They were of ballerinas, with wilting postures, large round eyes, and stunned, embryonic faces. The colors were lurid, the figures drippingly sentimental. I thought it was a joke, but my mother grinned and said, "Aren't they great? I snatched them up. You know me with my eagle eye. They're perfect for the room, the pinks and blues."

"I hate them."

Her face twisted. She sped to the paintings, her arms spread wide. "You, you!" she screamed. "What do you mean you hate them? I love them."

"They're Keane paintings. Don't you know what they are?"

"They're thin and you're not. You're jealous." She stood guard, her red knit suit clinging to her hips.

I pushed her aside. It was easy; she was never prepared for my physical assaults.

Once, on Luna Island, I shoved her onto the patio and locked the doors. It was winter, and she didn't have a coat. She paced and wheeled around, cursing in Yiddish: "Get shot. Swell up like a balloon and burst." After a while, she gestured that she was freezing, and we stared at each other until our faces melted and we laughed. My mother laughed so hard her nostrils quivered, and when I let her in, she said, "You nut. You really are a nut, you know that?"

I yanked the paintings off the wall. She pulled them from me and hung them up again. I pushed her hard and plucked the ballerinas down. I headed for the door, but she blocked my way, so I threw her against the wall. I felt I'd sunk in something oozy.

"Don't you *dare* do that," she said as I opened the front door.

"Watch." I carried the paintings to the incinerator room.

"Beast. Where did you come from?"

"Shut up."

"Stop screaming. Everyone can hear."

The paintings wouldn't fit in the chute so I left them against the wall, came back in, and brushed my hands in her face.

"You *didn't*. She looked down the hall, retrieved the ballerinas, and hung them up again, swatting at me. I ripped them down and threw them in my closet. When she went for the door, I pushed her hard, and she cried, *"Murderer!"*

There was a remote-control device on the glass table. I hurled it at her head, missing her by a fraction, hitting the closet, leaving a deep gash. I'd aimed as well as I could, but she'd moved. She didn't speak. I started to gasp, and I could see it scared her, so I kept doing it.

"Don't," she pleaded.

I sat before the bureau. My eyes were puffy, and my hair looked thin. I was fifteen, and soon I'd be bald. Bald and fat.

"Julie."

I kept heaving.

"It hurts me to see you upset. Remember when you were little, and I gave you butterfly kisses? You'd be sad, and I'd give you one. Let me do it." She raised her eyebrows in the mirror behind me. "Other mothers were content with regular kisses, but I gave special ones." She squeezed my hand.

"I hate you."

"You don't mean that." She sat on the bed, under the nails where the pictures had hung.

The first person I told was Lenny. I met Lenny on New Year's Eve during my senior year at Windsor. I was thin for a minute, and one afternoon in the Village, I flirted with a boy, and he asked me to a party.

Lenny was there. He was a freshman at Columbia, a dark, tall boy, restless and lethargic; sexy, I thought. He had a way of leaning close while listening and cupping his mouth when he dragged on a cigarette, releasing the smoke in a tense, narrow steam. We danced, drank, talked. He was going to be an architect and build "unalienated" cities. I said the city didn't feel alienated. It felt like home.

Lenny was a master walker, with a tireless stride and steady flow of conversation. He pointed out facades and ironwork, noted bits of overheard dialogue. New Year's Day, we met on Fifth Avenue and walked to the Village and my parents' squalid, accommodating Lower East Side. Merchants stood in doorways, hustling passersby in Yiddish, Spanish, English. We explored Chinatown, Wall Street, and Battery Park—then made our way uptown along the Hudson, through streets that looked like they'd been bombed. Trees rooted in the sidewalks grew tall and luxuriant; street people warmed themselves around trashcan fires.

Lenny's parents had urged him to stay in the Bronx, study engineering at City College, marry a neighborhood girl, and settle in a Riverdale high-rise, carpeted in wall-to-wall acrylic pile. Instead, he'd won a scholarship to Columbia and left home at seventeen. His friends wore wire-rimmed glasses and long hair that fell in their eyes. Lenny lived in a dorm room, because it was all he could afford, but his friends shared sprawling apartments. Grubby mattresses lined the rooms. Bean-crusted pots were piled in the kitchens, books and records everywhere else. Cats wandered, indifferent to the human tenants who came and went with the seasons.

Lenny said he loved me. He said it in my hair as we rode the subways, whispered it to my eyelids, lying in the grass in Central Park. Weekend nights, after my parents were in bed, I'd take him home. We'd sit on my mother's champagne-colored couch and strip, draping clothes on her mahogany table. Once she appeared. Lenny and I were naked, but it was dark and we were at the other end of the room. "Everything's fine, Mom, go back to sleep," I said, and she pivoted like a robot and went to her room. After that, I took Lenny to my room and locked the door.

I played with Lenny's penis, fondling its head, tender as a horse's nose. Lenny introduced me to orgasms. He was stroking me when I felt a tide, then a wave fanned out from my belly to my fingers and toes. "Was that it?"

"Yup." He smiled goofily.

Serge hadn't ruined me after all, but was my orgasm like Charlotte's, or the right kind? It didn't matter. It had felt too good. When I made Lenny come, he caught the sperm in a sock. After a while, he remembered to bring an extra pair.

We chose June for our first official screw. For the occasion, Lenny's friend George dispersed his roommates and put a sheet on his mattress. Lenny and I took a taxi, Lenny holding my hand, hugging me. Upstairs, we undressed and lay on the bed. Lenny moved toward me, his brown eyes filled with emotion.

I laughed.

"Stop it."

I closed my eyes, trying to get a grip, but when I opened them and saw Lenny nose-to-nose, peals of fresh laughter burst forth. He stared. I held my stomach. Then he laughed, which made me love him. We stroked each other, but Lenny moved fast. I was curious too, and as he entered me, I thought, "Never the same again." That was all there was time to think, because it was over. Lenny fell across my chest, and I cradled his head. After an interval I considered courteous, I wiggled out, to get a look at myself in the mirror. And that's when we saw that the rubber had torn. It had nearly disintegrated.

"Look," he said.

I was looking. Where else could my eyes go?

He loosened the shreds from his penis. "It broke." He kept stating the obvious, as if that would make it go away.

"How could it break? I thought they were never supposed to break. I thought you could fill them with water and drop them from buildings and they *still* wouldn't break."

"Yeah, the rubber ones. This is made of sheep intestine, the softest, the most like skin, the best money can buy." He stared at the pieces, unable to believe that something that had cost so much could let him down. I lay back, feeling like Tess of the D'Urbervilles at Stonehenge, sacrificial. Sheep intestines sounded biblical.

"Quick, get in the tub," he said.

"Why?"

"I'll get a soda. Acid kills sperm."

He came into the bathroom holding a 7-Up. "That's all they had." He whooshed it into my crotch, his mouth turned down. He looked like a kid taking care of a sick dog. I stared at the cracks on the ceiling. They looked like palm lines, predicting my fate. I'd get pregnant. I'd fold bras and girdles at Blumberg's department store. I'd die. My tombstone would read: "She never went to college."

We worried about my period. Worrying made us close, like waiting for a war to end. We were in Riverside Park, watching the lights come up in New Jersey, when Lenny told me *his* big secret. He took a deep breath and held my hand. "I never told this to anyone. I was adopted."

"Gosh," I said, although it didn't seem that big a deal. I'd spent a lot of time trying to get adopted. "That's why you're so much taller than your parents." Lenny was six-foot-three, his father five feet tall, and his mother four-foot-ten. Standing together, they had a circus air. I should have guessed he'd been adopted, but it hadn't crossed my mind. I'd thought Lenny was a genetic wonder.

"They swore me to secrecy. My father felt ashamed, a masculinity thing, I guess, or maybe it was my mother. I don't know who couldn't do what."

I snuggled into his armpit. The park was quiet, and the grass and trees smelled sweet. His heart pounded. "You should tell everyone. It's your life."

"Yeah." He paused. "But the secret isn't what gets me. I keep thinking there's this woman out there, my real mother. Why did she give me up? I figure she got pregnant by mistake. She was probably smart, and she didn't want to screw up her life."

"Like me."

"Yeah." He shifted so my head no longer felt comfortable.

"I don't see it that way, nuh uh. You're forgetting the war, the timing. Your mother was probably a refugee. Before she came here, she could have been raped."

"Great. My father was a Nazi."

"No, he wasn't. Forget the rape. Your father loved your mother. He was another refugee, but he died, and she was too weak and depressed to keep you. She gave you up, so you'd have a better life. Then she died."

"I killed her."

"No. She was weak for other reasons."

He looked at me with hope. "You think it could have happened that way?"

"Uh huh."

"It sounds awful." He was silent. "But any way you slice it, I'm not related to anyone by blood."

"Blood's not all it's cracked up to be." I kissed him. He licked my ear and cheek, sending sparks down my neck. He took my breast in his hand and teased the nipple, plucking it for a long time.

❖

I looked for blood in my underpants twenty times a day, but it didn't come. Waiting made us hot. Lenny got rubber rubbers, and every night we waited for my parents to go to sleep and tiptoed to my room. We screwed slower, and it felt good.

Lenny was on his back and I was straddling him when my mother rattled the doorknob, shouting, "Julie, Julie, let me in. What are you *doing* in there?"

We leapt off the bed as if it were electrified.

"Everything's okay, Ma. We're talking. Go back to sleep."

"Open the door this minute. What do you mean by locking doors?" She hammered and pulled at the knob.

The next voice was my father's. "What's going on, Thee?"

"They're in there, with *the door* locked." She sounded like she was talking about a murder.

"Julie," my father shouted, "get that door open."

"Just a second, Dad."

Lenny had whipped off the rubber and jammed it in his pocket. We pulled on our clothes and I threw the bolsters on the bed and opened the door. "Hi, what's the matter?"

My father's face was scarlet, his eyes wide. He turned to Lenny. "I trusted you, a college boy."

They came in and looked around. My mother pointed to a Chianti bottle on the table beside the bed. "They did it by candlelight." Her voice was hushed, as if she was explaining just how we'd committed the murder, Lenny and me: Leopold and Loeb.

My father's arm flew out, tracing a forty-five-degree angle. "Get out."

Lenny and I crept into the living room. My father's arm shot out again.

"Don't, Herschel, you'll have a stroke." My mother clutched her nightgown. "It's not so terrible."

"I'm sorry, Mr. Stark," Lenny's voice came from his feet.

My father looked past him, at me. "You. You made a fool of me." He pointed to the front door. "Get out."

"Aww, Herschel, don't." My mother ran to her room, came back, and slipped a twenty-dollar bill in my hand.

"Out!" My father's arm jerked again.

Lenny and I skulked into the hall, my father following, pointing at the elevator. "I never want to see you again."

I pressed the button, and we waited, but the elevator didn't come. My father looked from Lenny to me, from me to Lenny, frozen to the spot, his arm still out. I couldn't understand the heat of his anger. He'd told me sex was good, nice. I shouldn't do it because boys wouldn't respect me, but that had turned out false. I couldn't see, then, that the love between us had worked two ways. My father was losing me, the one who'd always been there and loved him above everyone else. The elevator arrived, Lenny and I got in. As the door closed, I saw my father, not moving.

We walked. It seemed I could keep walking. It was summer, and the air was mild, but I could not keep walking for the rest of my life. At Sixtieth Street, I felt wetness between my legs, and at first I didn't know what it was. Was I getting hot? From banishment? Then I understood, and the joy blotted out everything else. "I'm bleeding!"

Lenny grabbed my hand. "Whoopee!" We ran down Fifth Avenue, block after block, not slowing until we reached Saks.

The windows were filled with bathing scenes, groups of teenage manikins with reed-thin bodies and sultry faces.

"I have a secret I never told anybody," I said.

"What, babe?"

"When I was a kid I saw this shrink. Everybody in my family did. They still think he's Buddha. He tried to fuck me when I was fourteen."

"Really?"

I nodded.

"What did he do?"

"Stuff with his hands."

"You let him?" He looked shocked.

"For a while. You have to understand how much I looked up to him. Everyone did. It was supposed to be some kind of honor to know him."

"What did you do?"

"I got him to stop eventually, but I still hate him."

"Well, yeah." Lenny hugged me. "You'll forget him when you go to college. All that stuff will look like it happened to somebody else."

"You think?"

"Yeah. And you have me. I'll chase away those thoughts."

"Yeah," I said. I didn't believe him.

At Barnard, I met Connie Grossman. She lived in the dorm room next to mine, and I was attracted to her bohemian looks and bossy style. But I positively glued myself to her after meeting her family. Her older brother Marty was a senior at Columbia when we were freshmen, and the two of them often went home. Their mother Eva, a sculptor, and their father Karl, a pediatrician, lived a few blocks away, on 110th and Riverside Drive.

Friday and Saturday nights, the Grossman living room was a campsite.

All four Grossmans were tall and athletic, and they looked like each other, with high foreheads, large white teeth, and long fingers. Connie wore dangly silver earrings on her pierced ears and two silver-and-turquoise rings on her right forefinger. Eva was a redhead with freckly skin. She, Marty, and Connie were lean, Karl overweight. He would sidle up to a Sara Lee cake, begin eroding the icing at the edges, then work his way to the center, distracting everyone with his talk and laughter. He was heavy but handsome, with a shock of white hair that curled over his ears. He wore scarves instead of ties, even to the hospital.

Karl and Eva had come from Czechoslovakia. Their accents sounded smoky, deep, as if they held something delicious in their mouths. They didn't use articles. Eva's notes read, "Pork roast is in ice box" and "Leave keys on table." The Grossman apartment was furnished with dark wood pieces and oriental rugs. Sunday mornings, Eva would make her famous pancake, whipping egg whites into stiff peaks, beating yokes to a custard, adding cheese, scallions, and ham, then folding in the whites and slowly cooking the concoction on top of the stove. Waiting for it to cook, Karl would do the *New York Times* crossword, calling out clues. He knew the answers, but he hated doing anything alone.

Eva and Karl were descended from prominent Prague Jews. In 1938, when they were students, their families had come to New York to attend the World's Fair. They never returned, leaving behind relatives, property. As a child, Karl had been tutored in French and German. Later, in addition to Czech, English, Polish, and Russian, he learned Italian, Spanish, and Japanese.

Connie had the same laugh as her mother: hearty, from the stomach. I loved watching them pore over photographs, their heads bent at the same angle; or working in the kitchen, Connie washing lettuce, Eva slicing mushrooms. The kitchen table faced the river, and there we'd drink tea and watch boats. Eva called me "sveetie," the same way she did Connie.

The Grossmans took me skiing with them. Marty, a loping beast on land, was graceful and powerful on the slopes, ripping down a perilous run as if skimming whipped cream. Karl would get behind me. "Edge, turn, bend your knees, pole, unweight," he'd shout, and I moved, fearing to slow down with this bear on my tail. Eva teased me for playing the helpless female, because I let Marty lace my boots. I was Lenny's, but I liked Marty too.

Karl noticed what I wore, when I cut my hair, how I smelled. His greetings were lingering hugs, his goodbyes quick kisses on the lips. Once, when I pushed open an unlatched bathroom door, I caught him nude. "Sorry," I gasped, shutting the door.

"I'm not," he called out, laughing.

I knew there was trouble in the family. When I met the Grossmans, Eva and Karl had recently reunited after a separation, prompted by one of Karl's affairs. Marty slept too much and grew dull in the company of his father, causing Karl to feel ashamed that his vividness eclipsed his son. Connie was repelled that her father flirted with her friends, although it wasn't clear which she disliked more: that he was lecherous and appeared foolish, or that he spent on others the affection she thought belonged to Eva and her.

None of this diminished their appeal. The Grossmans were intelligent and warm, and they cared about the world. Eva and Connie were close and didn't exclude me because I liked men. But I did not see then what now seems written in neon: the resemblance between Karl and Serge. Both were doctors, with white hair and heavy bodies, who had escaped the Nazis. Both were erudite, had traveled widely, knew many languages, spoke with Eastern European accents, loved oriental rugs, and responded to me seductively. Estranged from Serge, I glommed onto a Serge of my own—a model Serge—not the charlatan who held my family in thrall.

Serge died while I was in college. I was living in a commune then, a place where encounter sessions were conducted regularly and cheese and peanut butter were bought in bulk. When my mother called with the news, I was in the kitchen, nibbling cheese.

"He's gone." My mother inhaled a cigarette. "I'm smoking again." She cried. "I never cry." She blew her nose. "He wasn't that sick. Stomach pains, went for tests, a stroke, *fftt.*" She exhaled. "It must have been the fat. Only seventy-one. Tssk. His money goes to Jerusalem University, the papers too. Isn't that beautiful?"

"Yeah." My voice was flat. I saw boys in yarmulkas poring over Serge's cases. "Lies. Everything he writes is a lie," I wanted to warn them.

I told my parents about Serge when I announced I was going to art school. I hadn't picked up a brush since the weekend at Serge's; at Barnard I'd studied art history. But when Connie decided to paint, I followed her lead.

"You're ruining your life," my mother said.

"I'm supposed to trust *your* judgment? Remember Serge, the genius, your guru? He tried to fuck me."

They laughed.

"How could you make up such a thing?" my father asked.

A mother-lion expression flitted across my mother's face,

then vanished. "How could you malign a man like that? He *said* you were beyond help. You really do have a disturbed mind."

"It happened."

"Gowan." My father waved his hand, pacing. "Serge? He was an old man. Maybe he was being affectionate, and you imagined he was doing those things."

"Maybe you *wanted* him to." My mother bit her bottom lip. "You were a hot kid. Some people are, some people aren't. I saw it right away. You wanted him to do those things, and then you dreamed it all up."

"It's true."

"Serge *really* touched you like that and you never told us?" I couldn't tell which thought disturbed my father more.

"Nah, nah." My mother smirked. "It's a good thing Serge is dead, so he doesn't have to hear about such things from a girl he tried to help."

"Yeah," my father said. "It's a good thing Serge is dead." But he wasn't, not for any of us.

Part Two

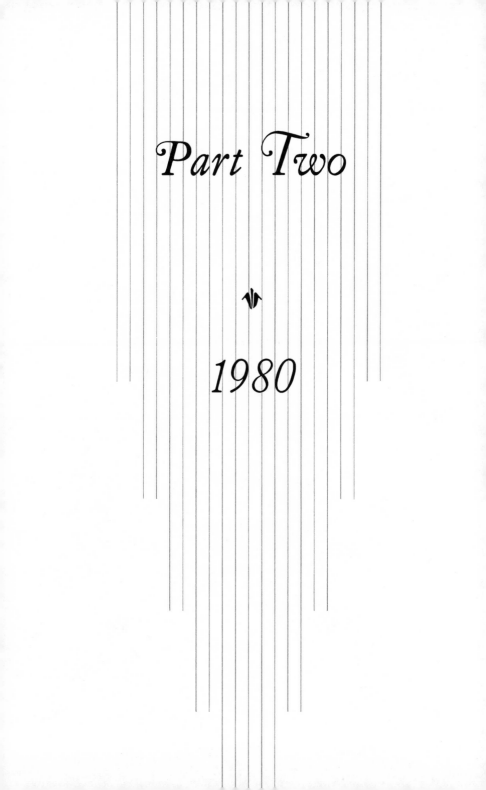

1980

Chapter 5

A MESSAGE ON my answering machine was the first sign that anything was wrong. My father always sounded awkward on the machine, but his voice was more hesitant than usual. I called, and he said he was "not good" in a half-wistful, half-dismissive tone. He'd fallen off a ladder in the Nutri-Pizza shop where he worked. Landing hard, he couldn't catch his breath, and he was so scared he screamed, which got him breathing again. He'd had X rays; his ribs weren't seriously bruised, but he couldn't recover his strength. It hurt to cough or laugh, and there was indigestion after meals.

"You've had a shock. It's natural to be tired," I said.

We arranged to meet the next day, at the sailboat pond in Central Park. I rode my bike up from Wooster Street. The June air was fresh, blanketing the city with optimism. But when I arrived at our meeting place, I couldn't find him. I told myself he got tired and went home, except he never got that tired and he'd never leave me waiting. I went to my parents' apartment, on Lexington and Seventy-eighth. I rang the bell, and he didn't answer. I banged and yelled, still no answer. Finally, I got a passkey from the doorman and went in. He was sitting on the couch, looking dazed.

When I'd last seen him, he'd moved with energy. He was seventy-three, but at times still resembled the father with the handball-playing arms and legs. Now, he leaned on me as we walked to the bedroom. His iron-gray hair was cropped short,

like a Roman senator's. His complexion was gray, and the flesh
on his face sagged, as though the muscles had given out. The legs
showing beneath his bathrobe were sticks.

"You've lost weight."

"Seven pounds, just in the last two weeks." He got into bed.
"The swimming. I'm up to twenty laps."

"Did you see Anderson?" He was the doctor we all used.

"I left a message, but he didn't call back." He waved his
hand. "The hell with doctors."

I picked up the phone and called Anderson. He said he'd
tried my father several times but hadn't gotten an answer. He
made an appointment for Monday. My father patted my hand,
his lashes touching his cheeks. I stretched out beside him, and we
kissed. I rested my head on his shoulder. "I love you."

"Not as much as I love you." He tried to look roguish, but
the expression came out a wince. "I'm tired, it's not me." He
shook his head.

I sat up. "What's the matter? You think you're dying? You're
not dying."

I thought he'd live past ninety, like his own father. I saw us
on a beach, salty and wet.

"And if I am? I've had a life."

"You're scared, and you're not used to it, so you think it's
death, but it's not."

He closed his eyes. I scanned the walls, covered with prints
from my parents' trips. They'd made it to Europe after all. The
prints were lined up edge to edge, like snapshots in an album.

My father opened his eyes, looking bewildered. He sat up
with effort and withdrew money from a dresser drawer. "You
said you needed clothes."

"Thanks." I put the bills in my pocket.

"You don't have to thank me for clothes." He looked at me
hard. "There's one thing I do want."

"Anything."

"Be friends with your mother."

"Oh Jesus." I hadn't seen her in six months. We'd make efforts to be civil, but invariably one of us would explode. Anything could set it off: Israel, a movie, a shade of lipstick. She'd criticize my life, and I'd make her feel stupid. She'd curse me, and I'd flee. Time would pass, and we'd miss each other. One of us would make a move and we'd try again, but we had no faith that peace would last.

"What is it with you? Still fighting at your age. Why do you care what she says?"

"Listen, Madelyn's her kid. I'm yours, that's the way it is."

"That's crap. I love Madelyn as much as you."

"Okay."

"Your mother loves you as much as Madelyn. She *loves* you. You don't believe it, because you think you're so smart, but she's the best friend you'll ever have."

"*That's* what you want for me? *Her* as my best friend?" I flung the money at him.

His face went scarlet, and for a moment he looked healthy. His arm flew out. "Go. I don't want to see you." The corners of his mouth were turned down. Twenty-dollar bills were scattered across his lap.

"Tough." I plunked myself in a chair, and he collapsed against his pillow and looked terrible again. He was breathing hard, as if he'd been running. I told myself he couldn't be very sick if this were happening. I sat on the bed. He looked frail enough to break. I took his hand, and he resisted. I grabbed it again, and he relented, too weak to struggle. I gathered the money. "I'm sorry."

"You're always sorry."

"I mean it. You know me."

"I ought to, I made you." He coughed. "Get me some water, would you?"

I let the bathroom tap run, the way he liked it. I was carrying the glass when my mother's key rattled in the door.

There was silence, then a loud sigh. "She's here, and she brought
a bike into this house. Why would she do such a thing?"

I went out to her. "Hi, Mom."

She was wearing one of her silk blouse, straight skirt, vest
combinations. Her hair was short but soft around her cheeks. Her
eyes were in shadow. But even at sixty-five, and even with the
lines disappointment had etched, she was still beautiful. "I'm not
your mother."

"I wish." I took a step forward.

"I disown you." She stood her ground.

I took another step. She stayed put, her eyes on me.

⚓

"I'll take him to Anderson," I told her on the phone the next
day. Monday morning, when I arrived at the apartment, I could
see tension in every lineament of her face; all her features
strained toward two deep apostrophes between her brows.

My father inched from the bedroom. My mother held out
her palms. "I've never seen anything like this." Her voice was a
little girl's, hushed.

I helped him with his jacket, and we moved into the hall like
an old couple. We crept into the elevator, then stood on the curb
while the doorman hailed a cab, my father watching, angry he
couldn't do it himself. We rode to Ninetieth Street and Park. We
didn't talk in the cab, or in the elevator, or in the waiting room,
and my father didn't want to read. Anderson strode out, his
bowtie stylishly crooked. He shook our hands, his cherubic curls
bouncing. "How *are* you, Hersch?" We could have been coming
for dinner.

"I could be better." His lips curled into a smile.

"You'll be more comfortable in my office," he said to me
and led my father away.

I sank onto his couch and stared at the photographs covering his walls. A young boy sat on a chestnut horse, his posture
ramrod erect. A woman with blue hair offered a measured smile;
she had to be eighty if she was a day but seemed vigorous
enough to chop down trees.

When Anderson came back, his mouth was straight. My
father shuffled in, looking brave and gray. Anderson scratched
his forehead, taking a seat at his desk. "His abdomen is tender,
and that's odd, because in March, when he had a checkup, everything was fine. I'm ordering X rays." He dialed a number. My
father watched, a child peering through a window. Anderson
made an appointment, and as he put down the phone, he raised
his eyebrows and let out some air. "I'm going on vacation at the
end of the week, for a month. Jonah Elias will be standing in.
He'll take care of everything until I get back." He smiled. "Don't
worry." He looked at my father. "Eat anything you want,
Hersch, anything at all."

The room trembled when he said he was going, but when he
said not to worry, I stopped worrying. When he said he was
coming back, I believed him. But outside, when I looked at my
father's ironic eyes, I knew we'd been deposited on a desert
island and Anderson had rowed away, calling out barely audible
instructions. I hugged my father, feeling how shrunken he was.
"I'll take you home."

"No, darling."

"I'll get you a cab."

"I want to take the bus." He tried to make his face look
strong. "I'll walk to Lexington. Who needs to hurry?" He inched
down the street. I watched until he turned the corner, but he
didn't look back.

The next few days, he stayed indoors, mostly in bed. I visited. When my mother came home, he'd sit on the terrace, and she'd pace back and forth, reporting news from the store.

Both my parents worked at the Nutri-Pizza shop on Seventy-fourth Street. Nutri-Pizza was my sister's brainchild. During the early seventies, she'd hit on the concept, catching the waves of fast food and health food, and the business had taken off like a shot. Charlie quit Wall Street and worked with her, but Madelyn was the one who made it work: hiring designers, cooks, serving staff. She loved organizing, inspiring people, and they did their best for her, because she seemed pleased with their efforts. Within the first year, there were three branches, and by the following spring my sister was launching shops across the country. She'd become very rich.

My father had already sold his business; the end had been painful. One day, he'd picked up the phone and heard Woody's psychoanalyst say, "Cut the cord now, or you'll never get out from under his thumb." My father hadn't suspected a thing; Woody's sunny surface had always beguiled him. When my father confronted him, Woody admitted he was going into business by himself. He dropped a second bomb: all the workers, except for Mr. Gardenia and Juan, were going too. My father didn't argue, nor ask for Woody's reasons. He bought out Woody's share, hired a new staff, and made Juan his assistant. But he'd lost heart. A year later, he sold the business. "Time for something else," he said, but there was nothing he wanted to do.

He lost money in the stock market. He was spiraling into despair when Nutri-Pizza came along. Now he served food behind the counter, whipping up toppings and lunch specials. He accepted a token salary. "What? I'm gonna take food out of my daughter's mouth? I can help her, I'm happy."

My mother, who hadn't held a paying job since her single days, manned the cash register. People called her "darling" and "sweetheart," pouring out their secrets, while her face registered every emotion. "Greta Garbo comes in. I make like I don't recognize her, then we talk."

In the Nutri-Pizza shop, my parents pretended they weren't married to each other, weren't even friends. "It's anybody's business?" my mother would say. "But you should hear the gossip. People see two old farts and try to fix us up. We have a ball."

Tuesday afternoon, my mother made coffee. "I don't know whether to work or stay home. Your father says, 'Go. I'm all right.' But you know him." She looked at her cup. "I'll go crazy if I stay."

"Go."

"He lies."

"He doesn't."

She screwed up her mouth. "Okay."

Wednesday, my parents went to the radiologist.

"How could they torture a man like that?" my mother said on the phone.

"They have to do tests."

"You don't know. He came back white as a sheet, and he was so weak. But they wouldn't let him go. They said they had to do more, so he did what they wanted. He said, 'Thee, I can't take this.' I told him to put his head on my shoulder. He broke down. They killed him."

Things killed my mother all the time: a late delivery, a bank statement.

⚜

Thursday, my father gave me another two hundred dollars. I waved it away, scared, but he pushed the bills into my pocket. "It's only money." We were on the terrace. He studied the clouds, as if looking for a sign.

"How do you feel?"

"Let's forget that." He smiled wryly, then poked the *Times* on his lap. "Ronald Reagan, that bastard with his Jerry Falwells and Billy Grahams. Who ever heard of a president so much with God?" He'd grown to hate religion, but he was fierce about Israel.

I pulled my chair close. "You're the best."

"You only say that because it's true." He looked weary. "How's the work?" He tried to sound casual.

"Okay," I said brightly.

I painted every day, and I was disciplined, but my approach was uncertain. When I started, I did abstracts: puzzle pieces I kept rearranging. Later my work grew figurative, and now I was painting narrative scenes. But it didn't matter what style I chose. I'd get scared before the end of a piece and finish hesitantly or not at all. Every time I headed in a new direction, I felt sure I'd chosen the wrong one. I thought I lacked talent, imagination, some crucial element. Afraid to show my work, I didn't.

"RAW did an action last week," I offered. RAW stood for Revolution/Art/Women. "We dressed up like paintings by women and handed out leaflets in front of SoHo galleries. We were protesting the tiny percentage of women artists they represent. I was an O'Keefe skull."

"Anybody pays attention?"

"I think so. Anyway, we gotta keep trying."

"If you say so." He took a deep breath. "And the restaurant?"

I worked as a cook at Blue's in the Night, named for Blue, the woman who owned it. "I did a chicken dish with jalapeños and a cornbread crust." I'd called it "Hester's Chicken."

He nodded, a parent indulging a kid at the sandbox.

"I *like* cooking, Daddy. We turned out to do the same things, cooking and painting."

My father drew bright swirling abstracts, using felt pens on cardboard. They were vivid, full of motion and feeling. They lined his counter and sold for five dollars apiece.

"You call what I do painting?"

"Absolutely."

"Nah, you take after your mother, opinionated. That's why you don't get along. Madelyn takes after her old man, practical." He sniffed the air, as if tidying his family had given him an appetite. "You know, I feel hungry. How 'bout a frozen yogurt."

"You got it." I raced to the ice cream parlor on the corner, afraid he'd lose his appetite before I got back. I brought chocolate, his favorite flavor, and when I returned he ate with gusto, spooning up mounds, rolling his mouth over them.

"Call Anderson," he said when he finished.

I dialed. Anderson's secretary said the results were good: The trouble was probably his gall bladder. The doctor would get back. My father hugged me with strength. He blinked, as if adjusting to strong light. When my mother came home, we celebrated, like it was New Year's Eve.

"Mama, Mama," she chanted, clasping her hands, shaking her head. We sat in a triangle, my father on the couch, me in the arm chair, my mother on a black leather seat—the last vestige of Stuart in the room.

"Show Julie my running shoes." My mother fetched them. "Tigers, see?"

My mother said, "Today a customer asked who I wanted to

come back as. I said, 'I don't know who I am *this* time around.' But your *father* knows who he is."

"Who?"

Her eyes narrowed. "Uh oh, the detective's out." She relented. "Go on, tell her."

"What do you want?"

"The past."

"I can't remember what I had for dinner last night, much less my childhood." But he nodded. He would have done cartwheels if I'd asked. He stretched his arms along the back of the couch, preparing to concentrate. My mother giggled like a disruptive child.

He could answer all my questions. His father's given name was Mendel, and before coming to this country he'd been a peddler. My grandfather had died of a brain tumor at age ninety; but in 1903, to dodge the Russian draft, he'd gathered twenty-five dollars and made his escape riding in steerage. For the first time, my father made this man sound clever, plucky. "He was from Kosnovia, near Minsk, or maybe it was Pinsk," he clowned.

"Everyone lived near Minsk or Pinsk," my mother came in. "It's like the Grand Concourse. Everyone lives near it, but I never met anyone who actually lived *on* it."

My father's mother, Shoshe, had come here in 1904, when Saul was two. My father said she'd been her mother's slave, raising a brood of brothers and sisters, then her own large family. "No one could curse like her," he said.

"Not better than my mother."

"She had yours beat by a mile."

"How do you know?"

"Because I heard your mother and I heard mine."

She shrugged, having to concede the point: My father's mother had died before my parents met.

"She was crazy." He shook his head. "When I was little, she banged my head on the kitchen table and broke a tooth. She never stopped asking for money. Saul used to get on me too. He had more than anyone, but he was a weasel. I had it up to here with him, so one day I socked him in the jaw, and he went tumbling back, like in a movie. I became the devil." He leaned forward. "You see, they couldn't stand that I'd gotten out. To them, I was a traitor. Saul they loved, because he stayed. He didn't give them a penny, but he was always 'The good Saul.' "

"How did your mother die?"

"Complications following an operation. It wasn't supposed to be serious." His eyes widened. "Gall bladder—well, I'll be—"

"A weakness in the genes." My mother said. "But don't worry. Nowadays such things don't happen." She knocked on the coffee table.

"She loved me in her way. She didn't want me to quit school. She thought I was the one with brains. You can imagine what the others were like, those geniuses. The poverty got to her, with no space and the kids getting sick." He sighed then began describing his father's older sister, a woman I'd never heard mentioned. "She was kind, and her English was good. I used to walk to her house every week, across the Brooklyn Bridge. It was quiet. She made tea and listened. Nobody else listened. She had daughters. Gentle. I took them to Coney Island. I'd stay late, and she'd give me a nickel for the trolley home." He dug in his mind for her name. "Leah." And then her children's names came back. "Rose, Bessie, Gertie, Sophie, and Mort . . . the youngest." He furrowed his brow. "Mort died young, only twenty-one. He was shot by the Scarlet Gang!"

My mother laughed. "*You* never told me that."

"I didn't know I remembered until now."

"I have a cousin who was shot by the Scarlet Gang? What the hell is the Scarlet Gang?"

"Seattle mobsters. Leah went West. The girls went into business, but the boy got mixed up with the Mob."

"How come?"

My father shrugged.

My mother said, "Go figure, your crazy parents raised you, and the nice Leah produced a gangster."

"Anyone could take a wrong step back then. It could have been me," my father said, tickled.

My mother moved to the couch. "Gowan."

"I'm tellin' you, it was a crapshoot."

She kissed him. "What wild lives we've led."

"It could have been me," he kept repeating, and my mother kept saying, "Gowan."

When Anderson called the next day, he said the problem wasn't in the gall bladder but the liver. My father was booked into Cedars Memorial for a week of tests.

Sunday afternoon, Madelyn drove in from New Jersey. I hadn't seen her in a year; we hadn't found the time. She looked fit and pretty, her hair swept off her forehead and waving around her shoulders. She drummed her nails on the dining room table. "What do you think it is?"

"I don't know. He was fine a month ago."

"Maybe he wasn't. Maybe he was pretending."

"He was swimming. He was working."

"He could have been in pain." She hugged me.

"I love you," I said.

"I know, doll."

My parents hobbled out. Madelyn helped my father; I held doors. Madelyn's Cadillac was in the driveway, and when she gave the doorman ten dollars, my mother stared at the bill. We got in the car, Madelyn and my father in the front, my mother and me behind.

My father looked out the window: at the Hudson, Grant's Tomb, the aging buildings along Riverside Drive, sights he'd

passed hundreds of times on his selling trips to New England. At
the hospital, his head swiveled. "Park on the street," he said in
his boss voice.

Madelyn coasted, looking for a space.

"Why don't we put it in a lot?" my mother suggested.

"It's not *necessary.*"

"Don't worry about the car," I said.

He turned red. "Why must you interfere?"

"Both of you get out and let Mom and me take care of the
car," Madelyn said, pulling over.

"I don't want her to get *a ticket,*" my father shouted. He was
panting, standing on shaky legs, smelling the air.

"Do you want to go in?" I asked him.

"No," he barked. "We'll all go together. What's the rush?"
He sat on a ledge, his face in the sun. My mother and sister came
running down the street, and he didn't say anything about the
car. Madelyn checked in, while he sat in a chair. His room was in
the new wing, where care was supposedly better.

He said, "I don't want that. It's just more money. They
think they've got you in a weakened position, so they can pull
whatever they want."

She changed the room. An orderly arrived with a wheelchair.

"I don't need that," my father protested.

"Hospital policy." The orderly was strapping and young.
My father shrugged and we rode to the eighth floor. The paint in
the corridors was yellow, the room we entered small and shabby.
When my mother finished unpacking, he picked up a gown and
headed for the bathroom, saying, "If you ladies will excuse me."

We heard water running and the toilet flush, normal sounds.
He emerged looking tiny, placed his radio and books on the
bedside table, hung his clothes in a metal locker. He got into bed
and folded his hands over the sheet. When an aide brought
menus, Madelyn read off items.

"Hard roll. Boiled potato," he answered like a quiz show contestant. "No TV."

"Are you sure?" I asked.

"I don't want that noise," he said calmly.

"Religion?" The aide asked.

"None," my father said sharply.

A young woman with long hair and tired eyes entered. "I'm Dr. Thompkins . . . Marian." She extended her hand.

My father patted it.

She smiled, tilting her head. "I have to draw blood."

"I've had enough tests. I don't want anything repeated."

"I know it's a pain having people poke at you, but everyone has bloods." She raised her hand. "I swear that's all."

We waited in the hall, outside the door. She came out, holding a vial of blood. It looked too red for someone very sick. "My first day as an intern," she said.

"Good luck," my mother shouted, as she sped down the hall.

We huddled around my father. When his dinner came, we watched him eat, a zoo creature. He took small bites, testing for pain.

My mother curled her lip at the food. Her chin fell toward her chest. "God, I haven't eaten all day."

"Take her home. Go," my father told Madelyn.

My mother shook her head.

"I wanna read. Go. I'm tired. I'll sleep."

She rose. Madelyn took her arm, suggesting a Chinese restaurant. I stayed. He dozed. Then I left.

The hospital was in Washington Heights, near our old neighborhood. It had seen better days. Chicken bones and pizza crusts coated the streets. Newspapers and food wrappers swirled in eddies. The shops looked like fortresses behind thick security gates. But the section was still pleasingly mixed, with Asian and Caribbean accents now dominant.

Kids were setting off firecrackers, and I realized it was the Fourth of July. With each explosion, I saw wounds and bloody limbs. I reached the subway: a dank, decrepit station. The only other person on the platform was a homeless man swathed in filthy clothes. He looked dazed, and the air around him smelled of excrement and decay. But he could still stand, and he wasn't in a hospital.

None of my father's relatives or business associates came. He'd cut the ties or they were dead.

My grandmother was dead, off in her sleep, amid ceramic poodles and palm-tree ashtrays. My mother didn't go to the funeral. I'd visited my grandmother several times when she was old. The last time, she'd insisted she'd read my mother's obituary. I told her my mother was alive, but she stuck to her conviction, and whether the delusion was a wish or a fear I couldn't tell.

Wolf had died a few years after Serge, of a heart attack, in his club. My father believed he'd been murdered. "I'm sure," he announced one day at lunch. "He was acting nuts at auctions, bidding on everything. Remember Cary Grant in that Hitchcock?"

"North by Northwest."

"Right. Wolf topped everybody, a manic thing, and he got into big debt with the Mafia. They had him hit. They have drugs, made it look like a heart attack. What kind of heart attack? He was never sick a day. That was his way, the women, the poker, the horses. Everyone got screwed out of money but Serge."

"What do you mean?"

"Wolf paid him from winnings, off the books, no taxes. I gave him cash too, the money I took in Saturdays."

After Wolf died, Nadine took over the business, and during the transition my father helped her, working without pay. Then she pulled back and stopped returning his calls.

"I guess she didn't want me around," my father said at another lunch.

"Maybe you remind her of Wolf. Maybe she doesn't want to be taken care of."

"How can you put me in the same category as Wolf? When she needed me she needed me, after that, goodbye."

"What if you wrote and asked why things fell apart?"

He shook his head. "She knows my number. Let her call or not. To me it's finished."

Neither one called.

Charlie came, also my sister's kids, Kevin and Molly. Monday night, Charlie brought a card signed by my father's regulars. He said, "You've got to get out of here. I'm counting on you for the new store."

"I'll do my best, son."

Molly gave my father a photograph of herself on ice. She was spinning, her arms crossed over her chest, her head thrown back. She was twelve and looked exactly like Madelyn had at that age. Molly snuggled beside my father, and he petted her hair.

Kevin sat on a chair. He was sixteen, a blond, polite boy, who seemed to be taking mental notes.

"You should see him with the games," my father said. "Oy, he once took me to an arcade. He's fantastic with the computers. This kid is fantastic."

Kevin looked at his father. Charlie was watching my father. We seemed like a crowd in the room. Madelyn kept touching Molly. My mother watched them, slipping her arm around me. My father said, "My kids come from good stock. I don't make losers."

But the next morning the spell was broken. Dr. Kraft, the liver specialist, came, Dr. Kraft, with his football-player neck and straight, unyielding mouth, said, "Biopsy," while looking at the wall.

"Nazi," my mother spat when he left.

My father shrugged. "Surgeons are killers. What do you expect?"

By the time Elias arrived, my mother was chain-smoking and pacing. Elias was forty: tall and slender, with short dark hair, tortoise-shell glasses, and soft hands. His breast-pocket hankie offset the burgundy shades in his tie. He led us to the lounge.

"How could a fall do this?" my mother said.

"It wasn't the fall. He lost his balance because he was already weak."

"I'm dying of schreck," she said.

Elias nodded. "He'll have X rays tomorrow."

"No more tests, that's what's *destroying* him. No more experiments."

Elias's head jerked back, then he took her hand. "Look, you know these things have to be done. His liver looks different from day to day. We're trying to help him." He looked at Madelyn and me. "Liver problems make it hard for people to eat, and we're concerned about his weight loss. Bring his favorite foods." He turned to my mother. "We'll do the biopsy tomorrow."

"Why not today?"

"We have to *look* at the X rays. Things are progressing as they should." He smiled. "We have experience."

"You pretend. There's so much doctors don't know, and what can we do? We're helpless."

Elias let out some air. "You're right. There are things we don't know, sometimes can't know. But believe me, we're doing our best."

"What if your best isn't enough? What if my husband's the one to suffer?"

"Do me a favor, take it one day at a time."

"*I* should do you a favor?"

"Do it for yourself. Herschel needs you to keep up your strength."

"There you're right." She stared out the window. "One day at a time." Her voice got faraway. "I'm alone."

"You have your daughters."

She snorted. "What good are daughters if I don't have him to torture?"

He put his arm around her shoulder. "You're a *shtarker*, you'll be all right."

She wriggled out. "Me, strong? Boy, have you got the wrong customer."

⇡

We shopped, Madelyn and I, at the Sloan's near the hospital. The one who arrived first would wait for the other, then we'd prowl the aisles. My father had quit smoking and taken to eating health foods, but that regime was suspended. We bought Haagen Dazs ice cream and Pepperidge Farm cookies–everything chocolate, like a kid's birthday. He could hardly eat. He'd spoon some ice cream from the container, but most of it would melt to soup. We brought corned beef and lox. He took tiny bites and sighed.

He could get from his bed to the bathroom, gripping furniture. He could sit in a wheelchair for half an hour. One of us would wheel him to the garden, and he'd stare at the roses, the brick walks, the spiky shoots of grass. Once, a yellowjacket landed on his shirt and walked leisurely across his chest. He smiled, charmed, a stranger in nature.

He read, either the *Times* or Melville's short stories, following my mother's New School syllabus. He slept. I'd find him on his back, his bridge in a glass of water, his mouth prune-like.

Over the years, I'd come to love his oldness: the soft white hairs at his neck, the sinews along his throat. Old men in fur hats would get on buses and I'd marvel at the delicacy of their cheekbones, the hollowness around their eyes. It's strange how the beauty of age sneaks up.

But my father didn't look old. He looked ravaged. The changes were so unbelievably swift I didn't believe them. I told myself people got sick, looked dreadful, recovered. There were pictures in books.

During the biopsy, Madelyn and I went to the cafeteria. She leaned her face close, and I noticed large pores I'd never seen. I breathed her in, her smell beneath the perfume. She played with bread sticks, making a pile of sesame seeds. "Daddy doesn't know me."

"What are you talking about?"

"He has pictures in his head. I'll never forget this. One day after Kevin was born, he came to my apartment and touched everything. He said it was terrific. He stood in the living room by the drapes and tears welled in his eyes. He said, 'Madelyn, you are a completely feminine woman.' I was supposed to think this was the biggest compliment in the world, but I thought it stank. He doesn't respect what he loves. He would never say you were 'feminine.' I didn't say anything, you know me. I just made Nutri-Pizza." She played with the seeds. "He still doesn't know what I've done. I swear, he thinks *he* manages the place, because I let him keep the books for one shop." She gripped my wrists. "You can *die* under anesthesia."

"He won't."

"Come to my house. Go sailing with me. See Molly skate. You say you will, but you never do."

"You've never been to my studio."

"You know what I've got going, the work, the kids, Charlie. Promise me you'll come."

"I work too."

"Oh come on, promise." She put her fingers through my hair.

"Okay."

"You mean it? As soon as Daddy gets well?"

I nodded, and she looked relieved. "What's with your love life, doll? Seeing anyone?"

I shook my head.

"I always liked Lenny."

My stomach tightened. Lenny and I had separated in college. It made me feel like a freak that she had to go back that far for a boyfriend.

"What went wrong?"

"We fucked around and told each other."

"Why didn't you keep quiet?"

"It was the sixties. We thought we were supposed to tell. He slept with my friend Sarah. She was hot for him, and I said it was okay, because I was sleeping with two other guys and I felt guilty. So the three of us got stoned one night, and they did it while I was there. I could hear them in the next room, laughing and bouncing on the bed. I wanted to kill them. After that Lenny wouldn't stop."

"That's too bad."

"No. We were assholes. We did what we did."

"Do you think about him?"

"Sure. He sends me postcards. He's living in Colorado, working as a city planner, married to a gynecologist named Michelle. They have a kid named Jessica." I sounded bitter.

"What do *you* want?"

"To paint."

"But you do."

"Not like I want."

"How is that?"

"I don't know. The ideas don't hold."

"You're afraid."

"Yeah." I often said this, but I felt it then, a jolt, a smell.

By the time we got upstairs, my father was in his room, awake. "How are my girls?"

"Fine, Daddy." Madelyn kissed his forehead. "How are *you?*"

"Oh, it didn't go so bad. I was only under for an hour. It really wasn't too bad." He seemed to have more energy. "Again they took X rays, always with the X rays. I'm so pumped up with radiation, they should drop me on the Arabs."

My mother peeked her face in like a scared child, then rushed forward. "Herschela, darling. I've been a wreck all day, the fear, you don't know. Tell me how you are? They knocked the shit out of you, didn't they?"

"I wish they would. I haven't crapped since Sunday."

"Him with his bowels, just like his father."

"What can I tell you? The food goes in, it's gotta come out. Nature."

"I don't care about nature. All I care about is you." She kissed him on the mouth.

He closed his eyes. "Umm."

She took a cigarette out of her bag. He grabbed it and tore it up. "I don't want to see that."

"I'm sorry. Don't get upset." She hit her forehead. "Where's my brain? Charlie sold two paintings." She pulled ten dollars from her wallet.

He waved it away. "We'll do the town when I get out."

"You betcha. Listen, guess who came in today. You never will. Helga."

"She's back?"

"Can you believe it? Your father and I know her for years. Tall, blond, money from the second husband, a plastic surgeon."

"A showgirl type."

"What are you talking 'type,' she *was* a showgirl. The first husband took her out of the line. She's still gorgeous."

"Great legs."

"Your father's a connoisseur."

"I didn't do so bad."

"So one day, she announces she's getting married to number four. I say, 'Helga, you swore off marriage.' She says, 'The young ones know how to do it: Sleep with 'em, but don't marry 'em. But I'm not young and this guy's old-fashioned, a European. I'll take a chance. I still got my own money, right? So she goes off to *Vienna, noch*. She sells her apartment, everything. And now, four months later, she's back. Different apartment, same neighborhood. She says he turned out to be a bastard. Like I'm surprised? Now, she's going to trust her instincts. 'I missed you guys,' she says. That's how she talks, 'you guys,' but she's sweet. She asked for you, Hersch, her boyfriend. 'Where's Herschel?' she asks. I told her you had a virus."

"Charlie thinks you two are plotting a coup," Madelyn said.

"Well, we do boss him around. After all he's not very bright, that *schmendrick*. Come on, admit it, Madelyn."

"He puts *up* with you."

"He has a choice?" My father sucked in his cheeks and held my mother around the waist. She lay her cheek against his. A few years back, they had almost split, my mother saying my father bored her. He went so far as finding an apartment, but when he got ready to sign the lease, she begged him to stay.

Little spots of color appeared in his cheeks, and I thought he'd live. We all did. We hadn't believed in something together since Serge.

Thursday morning, my father called. "I went to the toilet and blood came out. The toilet filled up." He sobbed, deep heaving sounds.

"What do you think happened?"

"At first I thought it was hemorrhoids, from straining, but there was too much blood." His voice rose to a whine. "I grabbed a towel and held it there. I felt too weak to stand, so I kept sitting."

"Of course you were weak."

"I got back to bed, and a nurse came in and cleaned me up."

"Is there any more blood?"

"I don't think so, but, Julie, it seemed like my whole intestines were coming out, like that's what I was shitting." He sobbed. "I'm sorry. This isn't me. I'm scared. I'm a goner for sure."

"You're *not*. You'll get better."

"Oh, darling, from your mouth to God's ear. I'm sorry I put this on you. That I should have to put this on a child."

"I can take it."

"If you say so." He drifted. "I'm tired, sweetheart." He hung up.

When I got to the hospital, my mother was in the lounge, smoking and staring into space. "You heard what happened? That Dr. Thompkins, who asked her to tell me?"

"She doesn't want him to go through this alone."

"*He* didn't want me to know. *You* have a stomach for this stuff. No one ever cared about him but me. No one ever cared about me but him. The doctors are killing him. They sap his strength."

"It's not the doctors' fault he's sick."

"You would take the side of any stranger against me." A stream of smoke shot out her nostrils.

"I'm on your side."

"God protect me from ever needing you. You think I don't know what you think of me? I'm weak. I'm beneath your contempt. I'd sooner put a bullet through my head than be in your hands."

"You'd be too scared." I looked at her through the stale air between us. "It's not going to do us any good to alienate the doctors. We need them, unfortunately, that's all I meant."

She ground out her cigarette. "There, you're right, my dear child, but I can't control my emotions."

That afternoon, my father began coughing and spitting. By evening it was bad. Every few minutes, he'd cough, almost choking, bringing up clumps of phlegm. To relieve him, a nurse used a sucking contraption attached to the wall. She held it to his mouth, and in a few minutes he felt better. Someone did it every few hours.

Friday morning, he cried when I entered. "I fell coming back from the bathroom. I was on the floor, and I couldn't get up. I screamed, and Jacob came. He's kind."

I hugged him. "He *is.*"

"From Barbados."

I laid my head on his chest, and he cried some more.

"Want a rub?"

He nodded.

I warmed lotion in my hands and drew back his sheet. His rib cage jutted from his smock, all the bones visible. I massaged his arms and legs, working his fingers and toes, the soles of his feet. His skin drank the moisture. His hands were purple from I.V. needles. He lay on his back, breathing hard, his chest rising and falling. Every few minutes, he spat into a cup.

"I want to sketch you."

"What is there to draw? Me without my teeth?"

"I'm getting used to it." I took a sketch pad from my bag. He was yellow from jaundice, and the bones in his head showed through his skin. His once taut, beautifully shaped top lip now dipped over the bottom one, making him look like a child.

"Do me a favor," he said.

"Anything."

"Love your mother."

"Look, we *can't* love each other the way you love us. Don't you get it?"

"Be her friend."

"Mothers and daughters always get close in time. Don't they?"

"What do I know?" He cried again.

∿

Elias came at five. We were all in the room, my father eating ice cream, coughing.

Elias sat beside him and patted his shoulder. "The biopsy shows cancer."

My father put his palms up. "The luck's run out."

My mother and sister clutched each other and stared at Elias. I did too. He said, "We're scheduling a bone marrow." His voice was clear, almost bright. "We need to see if the cancer's spread, in order to fight it. Tumors seldom originate in the liver. They come from other organs." He touched my father's hand. "The bone marrow test is no worse than the biopsy. You'll be up in your room in a few hours. Listen, we can treat this. There are drugs. You'll be able to go home and get back in your life." His lip twitched into a smile. "This is hard." He looked up. "For all of you. Any questions?"

No one spoke.

But I believed Elias when he said my father would go home. I thought he'd be sick, have to stay in bed. Maybe he'd have six months. I'd visit him every day. I'd be with him more in the next six months than in the last fifteen years.

"I'll come back before I leave the hospital. We can talk more." Elias left.

I followed him, a dog with a new owner. "Tell me something, when he was on the toilet and the blood came out, what did that mean?"

"We really don't know. Sometimes there's internal hemorrhaging, and then it stops. That's what happened. It didn't last long."

"He was very scared."

"We told him it had stopped and that it probably wouldn't recur. I think he feels better."

"Now he has cancer to worry about."

Elias sighed. "The weight loss is our biggest problem. He's losing more than he should."

"It hurts him to eat."

"I know. It's a bad feeling."

It didn't matter whether Elias knew things or didn't; he said everything with the same mesmerizing authority.

"How's your mother?"

"You saw."

He pulled a leather notebook from his jacket and wrote his home number on a sheet of paper. "Call whenever you need to."

I drifted to the lounge and bought a club soda from the vending machine. The bubbles stung my nose, and I remembered lunches with my father, places where the seltzer came out of spigots for free. My father loved to burp. He loved to sneeze, everything moving, making room for fresh stock. But there was no cleaning out cancer, was there? I stared at the sheet of paper in my hands. Elias's handwriting was illegible.

"He wanted to be alone with her," Madelyn said, sitting beside me. She cried, putting her head in her hands, and I touched her back.

My mother appeared at the door. She just stood, holding the frame. My sister held out her hand, but my mother didn't move. "I can't take it." Her voice was cracked, loud.

The others in the lounge looked up: an old woman with a cane and swollen legs, a young man covered with a crimson rash.

My mother repeated her phrase, and the old woman said, "I know, honey."

"Come sit down, Mom." Madelyn made room.

She kept standing. She lit a cigarette and walked to the window. "There's a dog that looks like Finn, the same spots." Her voice was flat. "Dogs are so defenseless."

"What kind of dog do you have?" the man with the rash asked.

"It's my daughter's. Dogs terrify me. I grew up in the city, and when you're ignorant and inexperienced, you get afraid of things. But this dog, I'm used to. My daughter loves him, so I love him. Know what I mean?"

The man nodded.

Finally she sat, leaning toward us. "He wanted me to hold him, so I did. He's so frail, there's nothing there, really nothing left at all. He sang 'The Party's Over.' " She shook her head. "Can you believe it?" I said, 'Stop, Hersch. We're going to Israel. You promised. You're not leaving me, you're not, so stop it this minute.' But he kept singing in that way of his, you know, big shot, sweet." She folded her hands. "He's slipping away. I try to give him strength, but he can't take it in."

"There's a clinic in Switzerland. Maybe Daddy should go. People have been cured." I saw him on a stretcher, wheeled into a plane. I'd tell him the clinic would work, and he'd believe me. Maybe it would.

"Gowan."

"It's true."

"He can barely sit up. How's he supposed to get on a plane?"

"Even if there's the smallest chance he could get better, shouldn't we try?"

She slipped into the haze. "I guess."

"I'll find out."

"Do that." She grew intense. "I'm starving." She ran a hand along her stomach. "My clothes are hanging. She looked at her watch. "It's six. I've really *got* to eat. But he wants me to stay. He said, 'Thee, I don't want you to leave.' The first time. I said, 'I won't, darling.' What am I gonna do?"

"There's a deli a few blocks away," Madelyn said.

"It's probably poison." She looked at me beseechingly.

"I'll go."

"Corned beef on rye, very lean. Tell them, 'No fat.' You have to say it, or they'll give you any old thing. Mustard on the bread, coleslaw on the side, a half-sour pickle. Make sure it's not completely sour, or it'll turn my stomach. Coffee with a little milk, no sugar. Maybe a side of potato salad? Why not? I'm starving." She pulled a ten-dollar bill through her fingers. I waved it away. "Are you crazy? Paying for me?" She pushed it in my hands.

It was the kind of summer evening that makes the skin feel baked and tight. Graffiti swam across buildings. The ice pops kids sucked dripped down their arms. At the deli, I gave my order to the man behind the counter, adding, "My mother wants lean. Get it?"

The man was about thirty. His stomach protruded like a beach ball. "Your mother and every other *alte cocker* in a ten-mile radius. First 'Lean,' then the wagging finger, then 'What's a matter, you're afraid to give a little meat?' I make a sandwich high as the Eiffel Tower, then I watch them take it apart. They can't get their teeth around it, but they're pleased." He folded a piece of corned beef with a practiced hand and offered it to me.

"No thanks."

He popped it in his mouth. "Vegetarian?"

I shook my head.

"Diet?"

"For life."

"A life sentence, huh? Wha'ju do?"

"I was a fat kid." At least once a day I said this to someone.

"You're shell-shocked."

"How did you get so smart?"

"You watch, you hear. A deli's the center of the universe."

"I thought the hospital was."

"You a nurse?"

I shook my head.

"Doctor? I should have said that first, right? Exposed my male chauvinism."

"Not a doctor."

"Your husband's a doctor."

"No husband."

"Oh, pretty girl like you, excuse me, pretty *woman* and no husband?"

"My father has cancer."

He was about to eat another piece of meat, but he stopped. "I'm sorry." He finished wrapping the sandwich and gave it to me. "You love him, huh? He's the one you love."

"You're amazing."

"It's your face. One face for the corned beef, another for the cancer, you put it together. Families. How many types are there?"

"Not many, I guess."

"You guess? You don't know?"

"I know but I forget, know, forget. Know what I mean?"

"Too much hospital."

"Bull's-eye."

Madelyn was gone when I got back. My mother was on my father's bed, urging him to eat ice cream. He swallowed, coughed, took deep breaths. My mother ran her fingers through his hair. He closed his eyes, and I gave her the food.

She opened the bag. "Thank God, lean."

"Eat, Thee." My father held her hand.

"I should eat? I want *you* to eat." She showed him the sandwich. "Look. The way you like."

He shook his head. "I can't."

"We fight, but what does it mean?"

"It never meant anything," he said. "Your family were beasts."

⋔

"We're losing him," my mother said the next morning. We were in the lounge. "They're pretending, with this bone marrow junk, just to show they're doing something. But no chemotherapy, I swear, Julie, I'm not going to let them do that."

The night before, I'd called my boss's brother, a cancer specialist at Sloan-Kettering. He'd said the clinic in Switzerland didn't treat people as sick as my father. He said liver cancer was a death sentence, although lives could be prolonged with radiation, diet, and chemotherapy. "Let's not rule out anything."

"You're with *them?* I'm going to have to fight you *too!*"

"Drugs can work."

"Who said anything about drugs?"

"That's what chemotherapy is."

"I don't care what it *is.*"

"Let's let Daddy decide."

"He'll say no. He doesn't trust those bastards any more than I do."

But there was nothing to decide. My father slept and coughed. Madelyn arrived, and the three of us sat in his room, urging him to eat cake and ice cream. We nodded together, listened to the doctors together. We became one ear, one mind, thinking for him, of him, no one but us knowing what we were losing.

"Auschwitz, that's all I see," my mother said the next day, She had a point. We'd come to the hospital then leave, and it would seem impossible that he could get thinner, weaker, but the next time he'd be worse. Saturday night, his hands began to shake. Sunday, there was blood in his spittle. Still, I thought he'd reach a plateau. I thought he'd last—sick and dying but alive. He could talk, eat, and piss.

Monday, his bone marrow was biopsied and that night he was given a shot of morphine. Afterward, he seemed better.

"How you doing, Mr. Stark?" Marian Thompkins said while taking his pulse.

"Herschela, darling."

"Herschela, darling," she repeated.

"She's about the right age. The rest of you, eh."

"Arr, Hersch, you said you liked me just the way I am." My mother sulked.

"I do, darling. You're beautiful. All my girls are beautiful. I wouldn't have them any other way."

"And what if we'd had ugly kids?"

"Then I'd say they were beautiful."

We piled on the bed, and it was like long ago, when Madelyn and I were kids and would jam ourselves between them. The hair on my father's chest would tickle. My mother's nipples would show through her nightgown. My parents could be so unexpectedly casual. On Luna Island, the night before our house was renovated, they let Madelyn and me paint the walls. In the living room, we painted our Washington Heights apartment and, in our bedroom, scenes from camp. We turned our parents' room into a beach, with waves all around. My mother and father egged us on, then joined in for the last mural. My mother drew herself on the shore, waving. My father painted himself next to her, his elbow leaning jauntily on her shoulder. I painted our house, floating out to sea. Madelyn painted all of us at the windows.

"You look better." My mother stroked my father's cheek.

"You only say that because it's true." He puckered his lips. She closed her eyes and lowered herself.

"Kiss me again," he whispered hoarsely.

Madelyn looked at me. I watched them. It was all we could do: Kiss him. He wanted to hear about the store from my mother, the business from Madelyn, painting from me. We spoke in turn, making everything sound hopeful but still waiting for something from him—a suggestion, a sign of approval. Nurses told us to leave, but we wouldn't. My father sang "Beginner's Luck," "Let's Do It," and "Embraceable You." His voice was a croak, but he could still sing.

His decline the next morning was shocking. A bag of glucose hung beside him. He was white, shrunken. His lungs were so filled with fluid there was a constant rattle. His hands trembled, the bruises making them look beaten.

When Elias came, he said the bone marrow test was negative. That was good, but still it hadn't been determined where the primary tumor was. More tests were needed. "It's rare, this kind of weight loss," he said in the hall. He scratched his head, then smoothed down his hair. "His liver function is so low he isn't metabolizing food. It's as if his body is eating itself."

We returned to my father. His head wobbled on the pillow, but he tried to sit up. He sank again. My mother gave him dividend checks. He signed them, then the pen slipped from his hand, and he was silent, except for the rattling in his throat. He moved in and out of consciousness, and we kept saying, "I love you."

By five o'clock, he was sliding into a coma. When Elias came back, he said there was nothing more to do except shoot him up with drugs. We nodded. My mother lowered her head, a horse with blinders. I thought the chemicals might work. A nurse brought a syringe that looked completely ordinary.

"The nerve," my mother yelled on the phone. "The nurse called and said, 'Mrs. Stark, he's going. You should come.' What does she know? She's a doctor? I called Elias. He said I should go at my usual time."

My heart beat in my mouth. I could barely button my shirt. I flew to the subway. It was faster than a cab, all that distance, the traffic lights. It was faster. I sweated in the air-conditioned car.

I ran to the hospital, ran down the corridors, banged my fist against the elevator wall. I ran to his room, pushed open the door, and there he was, on his back, his eyes closed, his eyelids quivering, his mouth open, no teeth, a deep, rattling wheeze coming out of him, his chest rising and falling. He looked worse—yes, it was possible, a skeletal form balanced between life and death. But he was my father. His top lip still bore traces of its sinuous curves. His eyebrows, delicate and high above his eyes, still lent his face its expression of wonder. I kissed his fleshless cheek, stroked his cold hands. "I'm his daughter," I told the nurse.

She was neat and unsmiling, around forty, brown hair in a bun. "Felice Charon" her name tag read. I stared at it.

"Anything wrong?" Her voice was tight.

"Your name."

"I don't understand."

"In Greek myth, Charon ferries the dead across the River Styx."

"I'm part Irish, part Norwegian," she said without irony.

I turned to my father. "Did he get morphine?"

"Are you a doctor?"

"I'm his *daughter*. I was just asking."

"Well, I can't give out that kind of information." She wrote on his chart. "I'm doing my job. I've seen a lot of people die, and I know the end."

"Look, I'm sorry my mother was rude. She's scared. People act crazy at times like this. Don't they?"

"Some more than others."

I sighed. My mother had met her match. "Can you tell me how much time is left?"

She tilted her head. "A few hours."

"*I'm* glad you called."

"I was doing my job."

I sat on the bed, while she threw flowers in the trash, took my father's pulse, cleared his lungs with the suction machine. "I'm here. It's Julie." I held his hands and touched his legs, feeling only bone.

"I need to straighten the bed."

She moved my father's arms and whipped off the top sheet, and that's when I saw that his gown had risen over his waist and his penis lay exposed. There it was, at last.

As a tot, I'd ridden on his feet, trying to pull down his pants. My mother and sister had shrieked, goading me. My father had let me make progress, but I was never allowed to succeed.

His penis was droopy but alive, still the color of flesh, a contrast to the rest of him, which was gray. I only saw it for an instant, because Felice, all nursy sobriety, quickly pulled down the gown and finished arranging the bed. "Mind if I take a break?" she asked, giving the top sheet a satisfied tap.

"It's fine."

"I'll be in the hall. Call if there's any change." She gave the room a proprietary look and stepped outside.

My father breathed arduously but regularly, and I fell into the rhythm. I closed my eyes, recalling a woman he'd once described from his traveling salesman days. She was from Providence, older and more experienced. She'd loved sex, and it had been a revelation. I saw their hotel room: faded blue wallpaper, a seascape over the bed, a small lamp with a green shade left on all night.

His chest rose and fell, and it seemed he could go on forever. Maybe Felice had been wrong about the time left. I would stay here, living in the present. Then I heard a rustling sound. I opened my eyes and found the room filled with vapor. Had the suction machine backed up? Was I enveloped in a cloud of cancer cells? The rustling sounded again, like silk brushing silk, and then a hazy form materialized on the other side of the bed. It gathered a shape, growing more and more distinct, and then I saw that it was Serge, wearing his striped robe.

"Why are you here?" I asked sharply.

"One old man is dying, so quite naturally you conjured another dead old man."

"Still so fast with the answers. What's with the clouds?"

"Death is a cliché, what can I tell you?" He nodded at my father. "So you got him to yourself after all."

"Don't look so smug. I forgave him for wanting my mother more than me."

"But you didn't forgive him for me. You're still on that bed."

I felt the old choking sensation.

"You think he surrendered his cock when he asked me to help his family. You think if he had been more of a man, he would have protected you from danger. Or if you were more of a person, you would have been spared the damage. But there is always more pain than can be accounted for. Look at it this way: I had the Nazis, Rivette had the rapists, you had me. I am the least of the three. Rivette and I would have traded places with you in a minute."

"So I'm supposed to forgive you?"

"Forgive your father. Give yourself a break. And ditch this romance with the cock. You grant it far too much credit. Since when could a cock save anyone? Masculinity is something men think they have and women think they need, nothing more."

"Now you're a feminist."

"I know what you know." He leaned forward. "Listen to me, let your father go. He has nothing more to give you."

I shivered. "I'm afraid."

"Get over it."

"How?"

"You are not small and puny. You will figure it out."

The door opened and Felice entered. When I turned back, Serge was gone. Felice took my father's pulse. "He's stable. Why don't you take a break. Come back in an hour."

"He'll still be here?"

She nodded.

I went to a phone booth, one of the old oak ones. It smelled sodden, as if grief had saturated the wood. My phone book was full of people I no longer talked to, some I couldn't even place. I wanted to call everyone, but I dialed Connie Grossman. We'd remained friends, surviving lovers and other passionate attachments. We'd said unforgivable things and forgiven them. She showed her paintings at a gallery, a good one, and her work was startling. I'd hardly seen her the past month, but she knew about my father. When she answered, I said, "He's dying."

"Oh, baby."

I cried.

"I'll come."

"Will you?"

"Of course."

"Now."

"I'm on my way."

I walked to the Hudson. Two cabin cruisers floated by and a large yacht, heading south, to the tip of Manhattan, maybe out to sea, to Europe, Russia. When I returned to the hospital, my father was breathing faster, harder, barely alive but still there.

"It's not long now," Felice said.

"Is he in pain?"

"He's unconscious."

She didn't know what he felt. No one did.

When my grandfather died, Saul called to give my father the news but gave it to me instead. I was fifteen. I sat waiting for my father in the den. I tried to feel sad, but all the time I was focused excitedly on the mission of informing my father he was an orphan. I wanted an outburst, something intimate, but he just pressed his lips together, stared at Stuart's green and beige carpet, and pulled his hands through his hair. Had he left something unsaid? Was he wishing he'd been with his father at the end and watched the serious, burdened mask compose itself for the

last time and freeze? He asked, in a distracted voice, if there'd
been mention of the funeral, and I said it was at ten the next
morning. He didn't appear to mind that I was giving him the
news, so I pressed. I asked if he was upset, and he moved his neck
and shoulders, something between a nod and a shrug, as if to say,
"I must be." His top lip protruded, but he was quiet, still, and in
that silence frustratingly beyond me.

I could see only patterns now, and I heard something tear-
ing. I picked up my father's hand. It was like a quivering bird. He
wheezed long and loud, minute after minute. Felice stood on one
side, I on the other. "I'm here," I said. He kept breathing. He
could go on; his heart was strong, and there was no cancer in his
bones. But then he gasped, like a sigh choking back tears, and a
steam of thick dark blood spurted from his mouth. Life went out
of him. It was palpable, a vibration hovering, then fading. My
father shriveled further, his skin becoming ashen, transparent,
his body growing insect-light. I stared, but he didn't look like my
father anymore.

"Let me clean him." Felice's voice was even. "Wait outside.
I'll call."

I stood near the door, one foot against the wall. The lino-
leum floor was mottled. I'd never have to see it again, or watch
people creeping through illness, afraid one false move would
lead to death. But I couldn't picture myself anyplace else.

My mother and sister appeared down the hall, a flurry of
movement, like a twister. They looked small and far away, but in
an instant they were beside me. "Why are you out here?" My
mother screamed.

"He's dead."

"What do you mean he's dead?" She moved toward the door
but didn't open it. Her face went blank, then filled with horror, as
if she were witnessing a violent transgression. "You, you, you.
How could he be dead?" Her head swiveled. *"Murderers."* She
whirled, flailing her arms. Madelyn caught her, and they cried on
each other's necks.

"I want to kiss him goodbye," Madelyn said.

"Not me." My mother shook her head. "I don't want to see him like that."

"The nurse is with him."

"What do you *mean?*" my mother howled.

"Cleaning him."

"What business does she have doing that? Do you know what she is? That killer!"

A few doors away, a doctor dropped his stethoscope, a young woman in a wheelchair laughed. I was too tired to join them. Madelyn went into the room. My mother careened off. I followed. In the lounge, she took out a cigarette. "It's finished, it's over." She walked out, and Connie appeared at the door. We hugged. I felt her long, taut form. She petted my hair. My body felt like wood. She held my hands. Hers were beautifully shaped, the fingers endless, like her legs. She'd modeled in college. Now there was paint under her nails. I said, "Blood came out of his mouth." She said, "How awful."

My mother and sister came in, my mother carrying my father's suitcase. "Check everything. They steal, those bastards." She opened the bag. "Where's his shaving brush?"

My sister picked it out and gave it to her.

She drew it along her cheek. "You didn't have to die. I need you. Please come back, please."

Connie went to her. "I'm sorry about your husband."

She stared. They'd met several times, but my mother seldom recognized my friends. "Thank you, darling." She squinted. "Why are you here?"

"Julie called."

"Why would she call you?"

"We're close."

"She's close to you. To you she's close."

I touched my mother's arm.

"Don't."

My head filled with redness, then black, and at that moment

Serge materialized again. He stood in the corner, holding a finger to his lips. "Shush. Don't take it personally."

"She's my *mother*."

Madelyn and Connie nodded, as if at a mute who'd learned to speak.

Serge went on, "She was a lot of things before you were born. You're just a shadow, a blur."

"I keep thinking I can save us."

"Oh really!" my mother burst out.

Serge pressed, "It's a vanity."

I folded my arms. "I give up."

"Finally!" my mother said.

"Go," Serge commanded.

I kissed Madelyn. Connie patted my sister's shoulder, and Madelyn smiled weakly. Connie put her arm around my waist and led me to the door.

"One of his slippers is missing," my mother shrieked.

"Go," Serge repeated. "Trust me."

"Ha!" I said.

My mother's face cleared, and she turned toward Serge. "She laughs at a time like this, at a time like this she laughs."

Chapter 6

CHARLIE CALLED TO say the funeral was the next morning at Fieldcrest Chapel. Connie came and my boss, Bertie Blue. June, Madelyn's secretary, was there, also Charlie and the kids, my mother and the coffin. The rabbi, who'd never seen us before, sent Her*schel* to God as "the devoted husband of Thea and the loving father of Madelyn and Julia." My mother threw herself on the coffin, arms spread wide. "Why did you have to leave me? Don't you know how much I love you?" She'd lost weight during my father's illness. She was as sleek as at her wedding.

The service ended in ten minutes. No cemetery; my father went to a crematorium. On the street, Bertie shook my mother's hand, and my mother said, "Thank you," her mouth forming a circle. She embraced Connie but didn't speak to me.

I went to breakfast with my friends. They had eggs, popovers, and strawberry butter. All I could eat was bread.

"Take a few days off. Hannah Dougal can come in," Bertie said.

"I wanna cook."

She shrugged. "Okay, hon. I just thought . . . but yeah, keep busy. It's better." Bertie looked butch, but she was soft.

It turned out I couldn't keep working. By evening, my throat was burning, and Elias sent over something with codeine. That week, too, Madelyn sprained her wrist and my mother got shingles.

I sat on my couch, feverish and achy, thinking about the ice cream I'd eaten from my father's container. I knew you couldn't catch cancer from food. I saw the image of myself as my father's death bride, but it didn't help. I was sure I was going to die. I stared at my paintings and kept seeing Serge.

I called Madelyn. "I want to come out."

"Great, doll, we'll have dinner."

She was at the station when I arrived, waiting in the Caddie. She beeped and waved, and I got in, sliding over maroon leather. Her wrist was taped, but she said it didn't hurt. We went to Brandy's, a posh, sedate restaurant: everything in peach. She ordered steak; I had swordfish—mediocre food, but we didn't care.

"I wanna know things."

She screwed up her mouth. "Shoot."

"Why did you come home from college?"

"I never told you?"

I shook my head.

"I stole a wallet."

I laughed.

The two of us thieves. We could have been part of the Scarlet Gang.

"How'd you get caught?"

"I flushed it down the toilet, and it backed up. Serge said I did it on purpose, to come home, a little breakdown. I was too dependent on Mother. I hated her bossing, but I couldn't stand to be away from her. Serge said I was stealing sex. You know what a prude Ma was, and she made me afraid. The wallet stood for pussy."

"He used that *word?*"

"Uh huh."

"Stop smirking."

"I'm not."

"You always do."

"What's wrong with pussy? Suddenly *you're* Miss Proper?"

"It's creepy, coming from him."

"It doesn't bother me." She folded her hands. "You fought with Mother openly, I sneaked around, and Daddy wouldn't stick up for me against her. Serge said I was more than Daddy's little girl. He made me feel worth something." She sipped her wine. "There's something else I never told you. I got pregnant when I was with Jacques. Don't look so accusing. I didn't tell you because you were too young and afterward it didn't matter. Serge arranged the abortion and paid for it. Mommy and Daddy never knew—Ma still doesn't. She would have made mincemeat out of me."

"Is that why you broke up with Jacques?"

"No. He was never going to please Mother and Dad."

"So you buckled."

"Pleasing them was what *I* wanted. Anyway, I wouldn't have been happy."

"Why?"

"The Jewish thing."

"Since when do you care about that?"

"A lot since the kids, but I always did. I just didn't know how to express it."

"What does it mean to you?"

"It makes me feel special."

"Like in chosen people?"

"Now who's smirking?" She pushed her plate away. "I think of Daddy watching over me. I sit in the car and say, 'I love you. I hope you can hear me.' I knew he wasn't coming out of the hospital. You were hopeful, but I was sure it was the end. It wasn't only the Jewish thing with Jacques. He didn't know whether to paint or open a jewelry store. Daddy knew what he wanted to do when he was fourteen."

"Did he have to be just like Daddy?"

"Uh huh."

"But Daddy didn't see your *value*, Jacques did."

"I liked the way Daddy lived."

"And you think that was specifically Jewish?"

"It was related. I want to be part of it. I am."

I took her hand. "Listen. Serge used Daddy, all of us. He was pulling the strings and laughing all the time."

"I don't think he laughed at us."

"You *know* what he did to me when I was a kid. Ma must have told you."

She nodded, and doubt flickered in her eyes, but she drew her chin up. "I'm not going to hate him. I don't. He got Mommy and Daddy back to the city. He got them to travel. He sent Mother to school and built up her confidence. She reads now. She's great with people. What did she ever do before but make sodas? And besides, Julie, nothing really *happened* to you, and even if he had done more, it was just sex. Why make such a big deal about it? People do shitty things all the time. Don't you know that?"

"I think we could have gotten better for our money."

"He was the person I had, and I wouldn't have wanted anyone else." She leaned forward. "Doll, you're always telling me you can't put a dollar price on everything. The way you believe in your paintings, even though they don't sell, that's how I believe in Serge."

"With all you know?"

"Yes."

"Even though he hurt me?"

"If you put it that way."

I turned away. Would I paint better if she said Serge was worthless? I dove into my food, eating everything on the plate. When I looked up, she was wearing her dangerous smile.

"Something else: When you were a baby, I used to steal your bottles. That's why you howled for food all the time."

I hadn't spoken to Wildeweiss since the weekend at Serge's. Occasionally, I'd seen him and Tana on campus, but I'd walked the other way. I called him now. "It's Julie Stark. Remember me?"

"Of course."

"My father died. I want to talk about Serge. Will you see me?"

I heard pages turning. "The Hungarian Pastry Shop, Tuesday at four?"

"How will we recognize each other?"

"I look the same. You are twice the age you were when we last met, so I will watch for someone double the person."

Tuesday morning, I washed my hair. It was short again: bangs, the sides straight and cropped, a helmet. I pushed back my cuticles, creamed my elbows and ankles, and stood in front of the mirror in a pair of silk tap pants Connie had given me. I still didn't like my body. It would never be lean enough, firm enough. I put on a black leather miniskirt, ankle boots, and a teal silk shirt with wide sleeves and a cossack collar.

I arrived at the cafe and spotted Wildeweiss in a flash. He hadn't changed. He was wearing a well-cut tweed jacket and a brown bowtie. His hair was dark; his eyes still inspected the world with tolerant pleasure, as if they'd seen the opera dozens of times but never tired of a new performance. He was at a table by a wall, positioned to catch all the activity. I waved, and he met me halfway. "You have become a woman."

The expression was startling. I called myself a woman, but in truth, to me, a woman was somebody else—someone Henry Miller had sex with.

Wildeweiss asked about my life, and I described my art, my job at the restaurant, RAW. I told him about my father's death, and after the waitress brought coffees, I asked him to talk about Serge.

"You want someone objective."

"Yes."

"You think I will be fair."

"Yes."

"Even though he was my friend."

"Yes."

"Even though I knew he was too close to his patients?"

"What did you think about that?"

"Many things, but I was not his analyst or judge. I was his friend."

"Couldn't a friend say, 'Stop'?"

His mustache twitched. "Perhaps, but I didn't want to."

"Why not?"

He smiled, and I could see little lines around his eyes that drooped down, despite the upward pull of muscle. "I could resist your questions now, but I don't want to any more than I wanted to tell him to stop. I was interested in what would happen."

"People got hurt."

"It's not a defense. It's just what I felt."

"But now do you see it differently?"

"My dear." He leaned forward. "Serge and I were friends for good reason. We had appetites for different things, but who am I to say he did more damage than good? Who are you?"

"I was a child. All his patients were like children."

"Alas, so was he, so am I."

"Confessing weakness, that's the end of it?"

He sat up straighter. "I would bet it never crossed your mind that you might cause me pain by asking these questions. I would bet that once you knew of my discomfort, you would tell yourself it was not important if it stood in the way of your desires."

"You have a choice not to answer."

"You had choices."

"What? To go to him or not, when everyone in my family trusted him, *worshipped him?* Besides, being curious about life isn't the same as putting your hands on a child."

"In a law court, yes, but in life, it depends on your tolerance for invasion. Are you forgetting you liked him?"

"Are you saying that makes me responsible?"

"Not at all. You had many desires at the same time. That is probably why he liked you."

"He didn't like me. He wanted to control me, all of us."

"Why not both?"

"You're playing with me."

"You play too. The way you're dressed. You came to seduce me. Oh, I know not into bed, but into giving you what you want. I didn't choose to direct Serge. I wanted to watch him play out his life. It wasn't an experiment. It was pleasant to have him trust me." A muscle in his cheek quivered. "He touched me. He was almost killed four times."

"The *war*. The war excuses everything. Everything is psychologized away. Can't you say it was wrong?"

"I already have. Do you feel better?"

I paused. "No."

"You hardly need me to confirm your sense of right and wrong."

I felt empty. I saw Serge kick off his shoes and pull me down. "What *do* I need?"

He met my eyes. "I suspect, to use your imagination."

"Show him to me."

"So you can analyze the analyst?"

"Maybe."

"He violated a taboo, so you get to do it too?"

"Yes."

"You think you'll get peace?"

"I don't think peace is what I'm after."

He stroked his chin. "Let me think about it." He flagged the waitress and ordered another coffee and a Linzer torte. When the cake arrived, he broke it half, then divided the remaining pieces. He could have gone on breaking them into infinitely smaller fragments, but every so often he popped a morsel in his mouth. It was one way of coping with the future.

"Do you remember Jacques?"

"I was wondering when you'd get around to him. We're friends."

"It makes sense, both like creatures from the Galápagos: no aggression, no natural enemies."

He wrote a number on a piece of paper. "Jacques."

I took it, feeling electricity. Jacques would be in his mid-forties. "How is Tana?"

Pain shot through his face. "She died last year, breast cancer. She wasn't surprised. She was always expecting death. Serge, on the other hand, thought he'd live forever."

"You have Jacques now that the others are gone. Maybe that's why you met."

"Perhaps, but the gains never catch up with the losses." He signaled for the check. "I have a class in ten minutes. May I see your work sometime?"

"I'd like that." We stood and I kissed his cheek. It smelled clean. He remained still.

⚑

A strange voice answered when I called Jacques's number, explaining I'd reached a shop called "African Nights" on Bleecker Street. I went the next day. Jacques was engrossed in conversation with a woman who was wearing a thick silver bracelet. There were lines around his mouth, but he was beautiful. When the woman left, I held out my hand. "I'm Julie Stark, Madelyn's sister."

He looked startled. "Julie?" There was still a hint of an accent. "You've changed."

"Had to. I was fourteen."

"No!"

"Madelyn was twenty, come on, you know."

He stretched out his arms, and we hugged. His body was firm. "How are you?" he asked.

"So-so. My father died of cancer a month ago. Wildeweiss gave me your number."

He pushed hair off his forehead. "How's Madelyn?"

"You know Nutri-Pizza?"

"Sure."

"It's hers."

"I think I knew that. Maybe from Wildeweiss, maybe I read it. But how is she?"

"Sad about my father, otherwise great. I guess. You know Madelyn. How can you really tell?"

"I could."

"You may have been the only one, or she let you think so. Anyway, her son, Kevin, is a computer genius, and Molly, her daughter, is a champion ice skater."

"And her husband?"

"Charlie's sweet. They live in a mansion in New Jersey. My father thought he'd have to support Madelyn all her life. He could never get over her becoming a mogul."

"I'm not surprised. She always appreciated money. The freedom."

A small man with tan skin and a wry face came over. Jacques introduced him as his partner, Tamar. We shook hands. "Hold the fort, will you?" Jacques said. "I want to take Julie for coffee. Long time no see."

Tamar smiled suggestively. I shot him a hard look, and his features snaked from their expression. Jacques let us sort it out, then took me to a cafe. He filled in the years—the lovers. He'd spent the most time with Karen, who was rich. "There's a pampered dog in me. Too much mother love, maybe. For Karen, I didn't have to be anything special. But nothing lasts. Right?"

"I like to think some things do."

"You like to save things. You wanted to rescue Madelyn and me, no?"

I nodded. "How is your painting going?"

"I stopped. I was never serious."

"I thought you were. You were my inspiration." I held up paint-speckled fingers.

He brushed my cheek with his finger. "What do you want now?"

"I don't know."

He took my hand. "You're beautiful, aren't you?"

"No."

"Let me see the work I inspired."

We headed east, past Italian groceries and bakeries. Couples slunk along, eating pizza and ice cream. We made our way to SoHo, past chic shops and galleries. I'd staked out my loft before the real estate boom. Up three flights we trudged, Finn greeting us with barks at the door. The dog trailed Jacques as he examined my paintings, spending the longest time on recent canvases. Women were plotting, sprawled on furniture, assembled yet vaguely distracted. In one painting, which wasn't finished, the women were outdoors. A figure gazed at mating dragonflies, her face rapt. Another watched a salamander slither over moss.

"I'm working blind," I said.

"It doesn't matter. Don't think about the end."

I got wine and filled two glasses. He sipped slowly, Finn beside him on the couch. I sat on a chair, describing the big moments in my life: wars and peace, sex and death.

"Come here," he said.

I moved, feeling hungry in the dimness. I put my drink on the coffee table, a cable spool I'd sanded and lacquered. He drew his hand down my nose, then licked two fingers and ran them across my lips. I tasted wine and lemon peel. He put one hand on my collarbone, soft, the other on my mouth. The hand on my neck moved to my chin, the other one cradled my head, and he brought his face to mine, first lightly, then his lips parted. I studied him in the shadows: a half-smile, the left eye sad, the right one ironic.

He pulled my shirt from my pants, opening the buttons. He pushed down the straps of my bra and touched my breasts, massaging the nipples. I opened his shirt, stroking his chest. Finn whined. "Shush," I said, seeing my father die.

Jacques kicked his pants and underwear aside.

"Stand there," I said. "Turn." He did. "Now the other way." His body was muscled, neither young nor old, except his ass, which was fresh out of the box. I took off my clothes and stood beside him, our skin touching but neither moving. We walked to the bed and held each other, kissing salty skin, exploring gently. We lay down. He took wetness from the tip of his penis and painted my eyelids, my nose, my lips. The mask grew tight. He slipped his hand along my thighs, up. Our tongues held each other. Our fingers slid, his freedom igniting mine, my hunger stoking his. He put his penis inside me, and it felt solid. We rolled, and I sat astride him, rocking, feeling him move up. He held my ass, and I stretched out, and together we rode to release.

But it wasn't enough. We started again, going faster. Jacques tasted his semen in me. I tasted myself on his cock. I licked his balls, the silky skin leading to his ass. He slipped wet fingers along the crease of my ass, moving in. Then he turned me around and entered, keeping his hands on my ass, moving rhythmically, insistently. I could see his face, sad.

I was fucking the smell of us, his skin. I saw Madelyn. I saw Serge. Revenge pumped through me in wave after wave, and as the waves washed up and as Serge became an old man waiting to die, I felt I'd had enough, for the time.

✣

Wildeweiss called. "I have letters from Serge it might interest you to read."

I rushed to his office and picked up the envelope. I went to
the restaurant, cooked, came home, and stared at the parcel. It
seemed like a lamp with a genie. Finn sat beside me, his head
resting on his paws. Suddenly, his ears went up and he leapt off
the couch, sniffing, prowling. A mouse darted along the floor,
and I screamed. It headed for the kitchen, but Finn ignored it and
gazed at me with my father's eyes.

I opened the envelope. Wildeweiss had typed the letters
and corrected the English. They were in chronological order,
some brief notes, others several pages long. In the first, dated
July 1955, Serge was on an ocean liner.

My Dear Wildeweiss,

I am happiest when traveling, for then being unmoored
and disjointed is normal. In New York, with my patients, I
forget how much I crave anonymity. That is not accurate. I
crave irresponsibility.

The ship, the *Philomel,* is huge. At first it seemed like a
labyrinth, endless tunnels and stairways leading to more
passages but never to the sea, or the dining room, or my
cabin. After a few days, a system emerged. Gradually, I
remembered a sofa in a lounge or a painting in a hall. The
routes grew shorter. The tunnels were, after all, connected,
and I saw that the ship was only a little island amid the vast
ocean. Now I feel cramped.

Chairs line the aft decks, where we recline, like invalids
on the Magic Mountain. I expect people to check their
pulses. The stewards, who are deeply bronzed, tuck in

blankets and carry food and drinks. They live by their smiles, but the beauty of the sea must be compensation for having to serve, especially when the fog rolls in and the pampered sardines lumber inside.

Sitting in the fog the other day, I recalled an episode from medical school days. I'd been studying depression and anxiety, and I believed I suffered from every symptom. I lost my appetite. Voices sounded muffled. My heart beat so loud I was sure other people could hear it. I went on holiday with friends to Switzerland, and still the symptoms continued, so I got it into my head that I was suffering not from anxiety but a fatal virus.

We were high in the Alps, surrounded by mountains I found oppressive. My room had a large window, which opened onto a balcony, and I used to leave the curtains open all the time, to let in as much light as possible. One morning, I awoke to see a dense white fog. It was so thick, pressing against the window, I couldn't see the terrace, and my first thought was "I've died and gone to heaven." I got out of bed, still unsure if I was alive. I didn't believe it until, at breakfast, my chums said I looked like a ghost. I've never again scoffed at visions of the afterlife.

Yesterday, I lingered on deck after the other passengers had gone inside and witnessed an extraordinary spectacle. Billowing clouds had obscured the sun for hours, but all at once an enormous window opened in the sky–a perfect rectangle–and behind it raced tiny cloudlets, forming a net over the sun, which blazed behind. There was a terrific feeling of depth and motion, and the sun lit the clouds with a light more beautiful than any I've seen. It was a sight one could only glimpse at sea, and I thought, "This is to compensate for Switzerland." You see, in my mind is a cosmic ledger book, in which I tally the pleasures I'm owed but none of the punishments I'm due.

The food is superb: chilled lobster and canard à l'orange,

coquilles Saint Jacques, crêpes suzettes Grand Maniér, as-
paragus au gratin, sausages, pâtés, cheeses, fruit baskets, ice
creams, cakes, wine, champagne. Already I cannot button
the trousers on my navy suit. Since this is what's left of the
ancien régime, I feel it my duty as a peasant to indulge to the
hilt.

I am fascinated by two sisters who share my table: Sarah
and Ruth, English Jews in their mid-thirties. Rubens would
have relished their overflowing bodies. They wear extrava-
gant *belle époque* clothes: strings of beads and hats with
plumes. They fill whatever space they inhabit with silvery
speech–that damn English facility for metaphor. And if
there is a piano anywhere nearby, they play and sing,
encouraging everyone to participate. Last night Sarah did a
rendition of "It's a Long Way to Tipperary," and I joined in
for the chorus, although I didn't know the words. I was
drunk from wine at dinner and got swept along. Most of the
passengers shoot the sisters dirty looks. They are the kind
of women who would be invisible if they didn't insist on
being seen and heard. I feel sympathy for their ugliness, but
I'm too much a coward to make common cause with them
openly.

Another member of our table is Gerald Norman, an enormous bear of a man from the Midwest, a true Yankee:
Protestant, independent-minded, living for each day with
no sense of history. He is twenty-eight, on his way to
England, where he plans to buy a wooden sailboat. He
knows little about boats and is prone to seasickness, but he
plans to restore the ship to its former glory and sail it to
America. There, the hope is, he will sell it and turn a
handsome profit. He knows he is risking his life, but it
doesn't scare him. He is charming and bold and completely
lacking in introspection. In the small town where he grew
up, his father sold insurance to farmers. Gerald was the only
one of his pals to leave home. (We in Melinka might have

stayed put too had Cossacks not stimulated our taste for travel.) I asked Gerald what distinguished him from the others, and he said he had never thought about it. He is telling the truth, and it seems to me his enviable fearlessness is the reward paid by his gratefully unprobed psyche.

I have been reading the infamous *Lolita,* and I can tell you that Mr. Nabokov is a genius and his book a jewel. It's not a dirty book as people say. It isn't arousing, but it is bold, for Nabokov makes the little girl the seducer. Of course the story is told by Humbert Humbert—a combination of humbug and pervert?—who admits to a fetish about prepubescent girls. His view of Lolita always serves his ends, but Nabokov makes both of their perspectives credible. There is no innocence, he says—not much, at any rate, past infancy. I do not want to spoil your pleasure, but I will say that Humbert doesn't end well, and my heart went out to him, because his knowledge provided him with so little comfort in the end.

We dock in two days, and I will miss my companions. It's the story of my life, but I can't adjust to it. I will write again soon, my dear friend. You come into my thoughts more than anyone. Do not work yourself to a frazzle. You have tenure, and they can't touch you now, lucky boy.

Your wandering Jew,
Serge

The next letter, dated 1959, was sent from Paris:

Friend of friends,

Your mother is dead. I am so sorry. How you must be suffering, although I am sure you aren't showing it. I have a vivid memory of your mother in her breakfast room in East Pauling. The sun was shining brightly and her face looked radiant—so much more youthful than it had any right to be at her age. She'd laid the table with our favorite foods, pretending she'd gone to no trouble. I liked her enormously, especially the fact that she wasn't relaxed about her wealth. It remained a mystery to her why the man she'd married became rich.

I've been thinking about my own mother, Beila. I know little about her, except that she was seven when her world fell apart. Both of her parents died: her father of influenza—no typhoid—her mother while giving birth to twins. The doctor was out of town, and she bled to death. The babies died too. The remaining children were then dispersed, and my mother adopted by neighbors. Her two sisters and a brother were sent to relatives many miles away, and she seldom saw them after that.

The people who adopted her owned a butcher shop and right away put her to work wrapping meat, scraping fat off counters, sweeping out slops. She felt they had taken her only to make her work, and from then on she hated meat. She could barely bring herself to touch it. In Melinka, we were considered vegetarians. We would pass a butcher shop, and loathing would sweep across her face.

"Were you ever happy?" I would ask, and she'd say, "No." "Did the butchers ever take you to Kiev?" I'd ask, and she'd say, "They would have if I had been their real daughter. But don't worry, they got back what they gave. Nothing." I'd persist. "Do we make you happy?" And she'd say, "Six children is too much. I'm used up." I'd put my arms around her, and she would pet my hair, but I was vague to her. We all were.

One day, though, she revealed she had seen a measure of light. From a drawer came two long auburn braids, wrapped in a silk handkerchief. "I cut them when Feigel was born." Feigel was my oldest sister. I held the heavy coils, shot with copper and gold. They felt like live snakes. She showed me photographs. In one, a white cloche sat low on her forehead. She looked beautiful, and it was shocking, because I could not reconcile this girl with the weary, defeated woman sitting beside me. She held my chin and pointed to a picture. "That dimple in your cheek comes from me." I looked at the photograph and then at her, back and forth, and for the first time thought I might be harboring some loveliness.

My mother died when I was fifteen, my father five years later, when I was in France. The rest of the family were killed during the war. I don't know what became of the braids.

I'll leave you now. For the crowning of de Gaulle, you must await my next letter.

Remember, your mother's love for you is your sweet solid core.

I hold a little of your grief in my heart,

Serge

Auschwitz, 15 July 1959

Wildeweiss,

I have paid my respects to my sisters' graves. Graves! What a word. I am shaking. Five women, their husbands, children. The line ends with me.

This place is more terrible than language can convey, and pictures of the dead are nauseating. A man at the crematorium told me a story about two sisters. The younger one was placed in a group headed for the ovens, and everyone in this pack was told to undress. "Put your clothes back on," the girl's sister whispered to her. She did, and when the guard came back, he looked at her and said, "You don't belong here. Get with the others." She was saved.

My sisters were the cleverest girls in Melinka, but not one was canny enough to devise such a ploy. I stood before the oven and saw each sister die: Feigel, Chana, Rachel, Lise, Roise.

Roise and I were like twins, except I, being a boy and a novelty in the family, was paid more attention. "Attention" is not the right word—let me say more was expected, exacted. There is usually at least one idiot in large families, but it wasn't the case in ours. My sisters were allowed to learn more than other girls, because for most of their lives they had no brother. My father was a tolerant man, with pretentions to cultivation. His father had been a milkman, but he worked as a postal clerk, the first man in his family who wasn't a laborer.

My sisters taught me to read. My mother thrust me on them, and I was therefore privy to conversations—their dreams and fears—usually kept secret from boys. It was as if I occupied a cavelike space under their skirts. Perhaps they resented me my privileges. Once Roise took a drum I loved and broke the skin with her foot. I screamed and ranted, and she was punished, but she took the beating defiantly. I am too sad to go on.

Serge

Jerusalem, 17 July 1960

Felix my man,

Peter Lewellen sounds intriguing. Go ahead and take the house with him on Fire Island, but don't let him break your heart.

The food in Israel is vile. Everyone rushes, and in restaurants one has to pay as soon as the meal arrives. Arabs are scorned and very poor. In their hotels, people lie sprawled on filthy mats, touching end to end. It's like a hospital ward in the Crimea.

But I love this country. I smile at everything, like a tolerant mother-in-law at the daughter-in-law's first dinner.

Wolf shares my sentiments. You should see his face when he hears Yiddish on the streets.

Last night I walked through the city, noticing every cobblestone and every item in the shops, singing to myself and smiling at passersby. The Israelis ignored me, but a young American in a cowboy hat lifted his palm and said, "How." I answered, "I wish I knew." I arrived at the Jerusalem Museum. Outside was a bronze sculpture: a young girl with her head thrown back, her eyes narrowed to slits, her mouth parted. Her thick legs were spread wide, and her hands were clasped and flung over her shoulder in a gesture of ecstasy. I cradled the head, which was round and hard as a coconut. I wanted to kiss her, but I was afraid I'd be seen, so I stuck my nose in her mouth.

At the Wailing Wall, Corinne complained that women are alotted only a third of the total space and aren't provided with prayer books. I said that she didn't give a damn about praying. She responded, "The point is that women are treated as inferiors, and I'm offended." Leave it to Corinne to know when she's not getting her due, but I saw her point. I feel happy in Israel, partly because I don't have to live here.

Regards from a Jew in the homeland,

Serge

London, 14 April 1961

Wildeweiss dear,

What can I tell you about love? It is never equal. You must let Peter discover his need for you, otherwise he will make you more miserable than he already does. I used to think I'd give anything to be good-looking, but I'm no longer sure.

For me, the conference on transference is mostly a social gathering and a chance to roam London. My enthusiasm for theory is waning. If I am to be honest, my energy for treating patients is dwindling too. Such feelings come and go, but it's disturbing, this depression. And the streets of London, in this cold, dank season, don't console me as they used to, with images of fellow-wanderers: Dickens, Carlyle, and Browning.

Yesterday in the underground, a woman lit a cigarette while leaning against the door of a moving car. She was powerfully sexual, in the way of some people who appear to be unconscious of their effect. My insides buckled. The cigarette, the lips, something about the mouth, the curve of her shoulder against the door frame—I think it was mainly her mouth. I lay my head against the greasy window, and when the train stopped and she got out, it was all I could do not to go after her.

I have not been able to get her out of my mind. Whatever restraints I used to exercise seem to be slipping. It saddens me, but it's as if I'm watching a movie about someone else. I'm willing to keep watching, but that's all.

Serge

San Sebastian, 21 April 1961

Felix boy,

I'm restored, peaceful. London was so cold it brought on despair. A history of the world should be written in terms of weather.

I took the train to Spain, rented a car, and for the past few days have been exploring the villages on the northern coast. The mountains rise from the shore, first cliffs and green shaggy hills, then majestic rocky peaks, which generate none of the claustrophobia of the Alps. Along the sea stretch miles of white beaches and tiny coves. Huge black rocks, battered by the waves and encrusted with cockles and mussels, guard the shore. People pry off the shellfish with knives and collect them, with greedy pleasure, in buckets.

Observing a tide pool, I saw a crab hide behind a rock, then pounce on small shrimp and minnows. I, myself, caught a shrimp in a glass. There were blue and red stripes on its legs, but the rest of its body was transparent. I could see its black vein and tiny pulsing heart. I lowered it back into the water, and although it had struggled to avoid capture, it did not want to leave the glass.

Yesterday, I discovered a beach which only surfaces at low tide. On the sand sits a cave that juts from a cliff and extends for thirty feet. It rises up twenty feet, and at the top is a window, into which the sun shines, and out of which shadows are cast, like a sundial. I stayed until the tide moved in, fleeing just before the beach was submerged. I imagined how beautiful the cave must look with the surf rushing in, crashing high, spurting out the top. But no human can see it unless he is willing to drown.

I drink beer and eat plates of shrimp, called *gambas*, tossed whole into bubbling olive oil and salt. Their black, shriveled eyes dart accusing looks, but thankfully, the heads come away with ease. Almost always, I am the sole foreigner, yet at dusk—as if this were a booming tourist area—children stand along the roads and hold signs in French, English, and German: "Rooms to let." I've found hotels, fortunately, for I could not bear to be ensconced with a family.

I have not thought about Nadine since arriving. That isn't true, but the obsession has abated. I do not want to let her go. I do not know what would become of me if I did. It's only here that I can stop imagining a future, but it's not here that I can live.

Your shrimp in a glass,
Serge

TWA Flight 117, 28 April 1961

Wildeweissnicht,

The Spanish peace gave out when I boarded the plane. I would throw over everything to have Nadine, and children, and grandchildren.

Sergei

Stockholm, 14 July 1961

Felixschiss,

Scandinavians have the least nostalgia of any people for religion and the most curiosity about evil. My talk on "Moral Sadism" was a success. Much applause and afterward good company, food, and wine. These analysts are more interested in group psychology than their American counterparts, and this sensitivity to collective good is refreshing.

In the airport, I picked up a novel, *The Spider's Nest,* a piece of pulp but it contains a bold description of sadomasochism. The masochist, a woman, is cured by psychoanalysis and promised thunderous "adult" orgasms. It's amusing to see how analytic treatment is imagined. Here, it's an emotional valve job, spark plugs all cleaned and shined. Would that it were really that miraculous.

I liked Peter's drawings. It's good you are helping him. Courage.

Sergei

Paris, 28 July 1961

Mensch mein,

I'm in ruins. I prowled the Sorbonne, and Miriam was everywhere. A dead pigeon lay on the street, its head bent sideways like a martyr. It was so large and corporeal I cried. My vision is blurred. My hands are shaking—my left hand has been trembling for days. I went to an art gallery, but all I could see was my own pained reflection in the glass. I could taste my longing for Miriam. I drank cup after cup of coffee to no avail. My nerves are wrecked.

When I was with Miriam, I was a human being. She was not a beauty, and for once that didn't matter. Her nose was long and her lips thin, but she had dazzling blue eyes. Her parents were rich socialists, and she grew up with few fears about the world. She made me feel that my suspicions were phantoms. We were a great pair: hope and pessimism, brilliance and shrewdness. I didn't mind that she was more original than me. In bed, when I held her, I felt her powers seeping under my skin. I felt young for the only time in my life, that sense of promise and inexhaustible vigor, the feeling that your time is the best one possible and can shape the future.

She'd drag me to movies and plays. If we went to a political meeting, she'd fall asleep on my shoulder, then, as soon as it was over, awake, full of energy. Mostly we walked and talked. Is there anything more inspiring than a great city beneath your feet and a tireless trekker by your side? Everything seems large and new. You think you will discover the structure beneath all systems and never exhaust conversation. Maybe I wouldn't have run out of spirit if she had lived.

She loved talking about psychoanalysis, but even more she loved the process with her patients. She made psychoanalysis sound like a large humanizing enterprise. "When God died, people lost the pleasure of believing in a higher authority. Our job is to show them the pleasures of consciousness," she used to say. She saw analysis as part of democracy—every psyche being as complex and interesting as all others—and she thought that everyone could become wiser through self-scrutiny.

The war did not change her mind. She knew that people yearned to follow leaders, and she thought she understood why. It was their longing for received formulas—ideas about people and society untested against their own experience. This longing was a failure of the imagination, of empathy, she said. She gave irrationality its due, but perhaps because she hated it so much she did not regard it with sufficient seriousness. Perhaps if she had known fear and cowardice as intimately as I, she would have survived.

She thought Jews should stay in Europe and fight. In any case, she wouldn't leave her parents. Her father was ill and couldn't travel. She said she would meet me in Casablanca when the time was right, but she never made it. Friends wrote when she was arrested. She died in Bergen-Belsen.

How long did I have to be human? Two years? Two and a half if I count from the time I first saw her in neurology class, twirling her long, fine hair.

The hair of women I loved floats through Europe.

As always,
Serge

Amsterdam, 2 August 1961
Wildeweiss,

Nadine put her hand on my arm: "If I were going to take a lover, it would be you. You are the only man I have ever trusted. But if I slept with you, that would end my trust, and I couldn't bear it." She was as graceful as anyone could be turning down a worshipper. She is the quintessence of gentleness and resourcefulness, a beauty who was once plain, a creature pressed by her father but not broken.

A few days after she arrived, the hordes came: Wolf, Bliss, Corinne, Ames, and Tana. I look at Bliss, shrouded in her Bergdorf finery, and see a concentration camp body. A fitting irony for the Jews.

I am crumbling, but they do not know. The buzz of their needs seduces me into life.

Serge

Dubrovnik, 30 July 1962

Mensch,

Last night I dreamed my father had died. In the dream, no one liked him, including his wife, who did not look like my mother but who, like my mother, was happy to be rid of him. He had been a genius *manqué* and had killed himself, but whether by intent or accident was uncertain. He had been a secret agent, and while attempting to blow up a building had enmeshed himself in the fuses and been blown apart. I did not see his remains, but I was told that his bottom part–the torso and legs–were intact, still clothed, and frozen in a bicycle-riding position.

The funeral was a fiasco, with an assortment of people who acted contemptuous. I didn't cry at first, but after seeing how cold everyone was, I burst into a torrent of tears and went around to each person, extolling my father's virtues and defending his honor. In the course of this endeavor, I realized that I, too, was dead, although in a different way. I was still conscious and could communicate with people, but I could only be a spectator. I could no longer change myself or affect others. A boyhood friend, Shmul, was at the funeral. When he heard I was dead, he laughed slowly and ironically, and there was nothing I could do to alter his opinion.

Throughout the dream, I felt pained about being cut off before my time. I wondered if I might be dreaming but couldn't convince myself that was the case. Half an hour ago I awoke with enormous relief.

Here is my interpretation: I was dreaming about my own death twice. In the first case I was reckless, in the second a passive victim: my two sides. In the dream, I am the only one who minds that I am dead. I am telling myself I love life more than I usually admit.

Corinne and Ames arrive tomorrow, and I will show them the ancient walled regions of Dubrovnik. We have so much money it embarrasses me, especially in the inland villages where people are very poor.

Congratulations on the Craig-Fortnam prize! I knew you were a genius, but it's pleasing to see the world agree.

Your Russian bear,
Sergeievich

Avignon, 22 November 1963

Felix,

Kennedy dead. I am shaking with shock and disappointment. The French are talking, but they do not feel the grief. I believed in this man. America has always had a wild streak: the West, the frontier, but something more sinister has developed. I thought I had come to a new world. It's not the first time I was wrong.

Serge

Park Avenue, 25 December 1964

Wildeweiss mein mensch,

A mathematics conference in the Bahamas! I can picture the lot of you, proving the uncertainty principle while debating whether to meet in the sun or in the shade!

My dining room chairs arrived Friday and the apartment is complete. Alas, it doesn't feel that way. The rugs are all that's left of the old place. I step on them, like stones on a path, thinking they will lead to some place familiar, but they don't. With the glass and chrome and marble everywhere, it's like a skyscraper inside. I am New Yorker now, for sure, ya, ya.

Every day I work two hours on the essay about architecture and dreams. Do you suppose this article relates to my renovations? Ahem.

Tonight I go to Tana's for goose, presents, and Europeans. Tana wishes I would love her. If I did, it would solve many problems, so of course I cannot.

American Jews think Christmas is a Nazi plot. Thea especially amuses me. With no real Nazis around, she finds them under every rock. Only in a free society can paranoia stand out in such clear relief.

Wolf blasted me for "giving Corinne to Ames." I said, "If I were the kind of doctor who told her to wait for her lover, you would be a fool to pay me for treating you." He said, "Get shot. Have a heart attack. Get run over by an oxcart." All Starks curse the same.

It has never been clear whether the analyst is master of the analytic enterprise or a hireling. It seems to me my patients have helped me more than I them. I look at Herschel, so moved by the past yet hating it, seeing in it only disorder and violence. Wolf is the opposite. His reverence for the past—expressed in his love of antiques—keeps him sane. I envy Ames too. All these handsome men with money and lovely women. I am their war orphan.

Good Shabbos,
Serge

Park Avenue, 13 June 1966

Dear Friend,

I do not like this business in Vietnam. For the French it was a quagmire, just like Algeria. When you return from your decadent debauch—massages, boys, hashish—I will enlist your aid for a letter to President Johnson.

Today I am sixty-five. I stood naked in front of the mirror and almost had a heart attack.

New York asks for you,

Sergei

Vienna, 12 August 1968

Friend,

Freud's apartment is merely a shell, for most of the furniture is in London. But the tranquil garden still blooms,

and the rooms are suffused with an atmosphere of seriousness and pain that went right through me. Freud spent more
than fifty years working here. On the walls are photographs, memorabilia, bits of writing from letters and articles. Everywhere I could feel his desire to force candor
upon his resistant psyche. I felt ashamed.

Serge

Mount Sinai Hospital, 18 May 1969
Dear Felix,

At the moment, there is no pain, and I suspect my problem is nothing more serious than an ulcer. I've lost five
pounds, and I rejoice, but I'd rather be reducing at a spa.

Wolf brought chocolate truffles from Belgium, knowing I
love them, forgetting I cannot eat them. Nadine brought
calla lilies, champagne roses, and tulips. Their insides look
like sex. I close my eyes thinking I will sleep, and I see
naked bodies.

I was always glimpsing spots of blood on my sisters'
clothes, wondering what they meant. Their eyes would dart
away when they saw me snooping. I shared a bed with Lise
and Roise until I was five. They played with me like a doll,
but I was too little to have the same freedom with them.
They would put me between them and on cold nights warm
their feet on my skin. I shrieked but liked it.

A few days after my Bar Mitzvah, a girl named Ella took
me into the woods. She was sixteen, already a woman, but
odd and quiet, and she let me fondle her breasts and put my
fingers inside her. I thought it was a gift from God for
reciting my Haftorah so well.

After the war started, I wanted to stay in bed all the time.
It was a miracle I arrived for any of my appointments. I
would arrange liaisons in my office, between patients. The
time constraints excited me. I loved whoever was in my

arms, simply because she wanted me, or gave in to me. I saw patients between bouts of sex. I had sex with patients.

There is nothing in this world like the romance between the analyst and patient. The best analysts, like Zen masters, feel pleasure in restraint, in allowing the drama to unfold rather than shaping it, in letting Platonic love do the work of untangling, never bringing flesh to flesh. For a great analyst, there is but a tiny audience of two: the analyst and patient, for no one else can see what they accomplish.

I was never able to stand that obscurity. I said too much, showed off. I have been an immigrant since I was eighteen, not knowing my place—not in my own family, not in the world—unable to bear being outside. In Europe, I saw sacred taboos sundered in the world's hatred of Jews. "What could *I* do that would matter?" I rationalized. These words didn't precisely form in my mind, but they were inside me. There were few female patients I did not try to seduce, and with most I succeeded because the analyst's role makes him so powerful. I told myself my actions were not crimes. Of course, the fact that they were—and that I was the provocateur rather than the passive victim—was what excited me.

The problem was inside me in Europe, but I was young and promising and not so alone. In America, I ran amok. It's the simple truth.

Sex remains as tempting as ever. This morning, I awoke with a hard-on.

Good night,
Serge

This, the last letter, was written the day before he died.

My eyes flooded, and the room became blurred, a Monet. I blinked, brushing away the tears, and when I opened my eyes, Serge was across from me, still in his robe.

"Don't you ever get dressed?"

"This is as formal as it gets."

"Why are you back?"

"To say goodbye." He leaned forward. "I have no other secrets, except to say that you must throw yourself into work until you lose all self-consciousness." His arms were out, something between a shrug and a gesture of welcome.

I didn't want him to go, but he was fading, searching my face for a farewell with which I could live and he could stay dead.

"Good night," I said.

He smiled, his eyebrows rising to half moons, his cheeks inflating in that way of his that showed he was pleased. Then he was nothing, and my head filled with fog.

⁂

A few weeks later, my mother and I met in Caffe Tartuffo. She'd brought my father's ashes. They were in a copper capsule, shaped like a large bullet. "I talk to it all the time. It's no good. You have to keep it." The bullet was in a Bloomingdale's shopping bag; Bloomingdale's had been one of my father's most lucrative accounts. My mother put the bag on her lap, then on the table, but it took up so much room we couldn't see each other. Finally, she placed it under the table, between our legs.

She lit a cigarette, then grabbed my hair. "My God, it's gray, you've got a gray hair."

"It's not the first."

"I've never heard of anyone your age with a gray hair. I never had one. Your father never did until he was much, much older. Your sister doesn't have any now. You must do a lot of worrying."

I shrugged.

"Gray hair's gotta mean something. Maybe you're not eating right."

"I'm a *cook*."

"Don't remind me."

A waitress came to the table, a pretty young black woman, who sniffled.

"You have a cold, darling?"

"Yeah, and I'm beat."

My mother opened her purse and handed the woman two tissues and a hard candy.

"What a nice thing."

She waved her hand. "Just human."

The waitress motioned to the room. "To them I'm someone to bring rolls."

"My whole life I carried rolls. You with seeds, me with onions."

She laughed. "You're funny."

My mother shook her head. "I'm funny to strangers, to strangers I'm funny." She put on a pleading face and tapped the menu. "I know there's a minimum, darling, but I'm not hungry. I recently suffered a terrible loss."

"What happened?"

"My husband. Forty-five years."

"Your husband was forty-five?"

My mother cracked up, her nostrils quivering. "I was *married* forty-five years. What a riot, me with a man that young."

"You could, honey. You look good."

"You're a sweetheart."

"Honey, eat what you want." The waitress winked. "I'll take care of it."

I ordered shrimp salad and coffee, my mother just coffee.

She brushed at my hair again. "The queers you hang out with. Blue. Who ever heard of such a name?"

"It comes from Blumenthal."

"A Jew?" She shook her head. "That Jews should have to live with such a thing. At least I don't have *that.*" She stared into space and tapped my hand. "But it's not your fault you're the way you are. The sixties ruined you." She looked me in the eye. "Don't laugh. I'm telling the truth. Then again, why not laugh? I cry buckets. I never used to cry. Now all I do is sob. My nose runs. People think I take cocaine. I see your father on the street, with his walk, you know, speedy, always running for a bus even when he wasn't. And with that hat, you know with the peak? I see the hat, and I'm finished."

"You have the work."

"Without that I'd shoot myself. But inside." She beat her chest. "What can I say? Today, at the cash register, my hands looked like paper." She stared at Signora Danello, the owner of the cafe, a tall, broad-shouldered woman who was leaning over the counter. "My mother used to stand like that. She never sat down." She lit another cigarette and inhaled, letting the smoke out slow. Her tone was quiet. "She tried in her way. She made me such a room out of a closet, no windows, just big enough for a bed. That's how bad I wanted privacy. My brothers used to attack me, the three of them. My mother let them, because they were her men. My father was never home, always working. I couldn't bring a friend in the house. Duddy once threw his razor and sliced my lip." She pointed to a thin scar running to her nose. She looked dazed, but there was room—a closet—in her mood. It was as if the harm she'd long feared had come in the form of my father's death. Having survived it, she was free to speak.

"Before you had the room, where did you sleep?" I asked.

"All the kids together, you know, a tenement, two rooms and the kitchen."

"And did the brothers come to your bed?"

She nodded calmly. "First Duddy, then the others, when they saw nothing would happen."

"And did they touch you?"

She nodded.

"Did they enter you?"

She shook her head, then shrugged. "I don't think so, too scared for that, just rubbed against, I don't know." She paused. "They put their hands and mouths on me, all over. They made me touch them, threatened to tell if I didn't, and I was too stupid to understand they were lying."

Another day, she was going on about my father, and I said I missed Wolf.

She exploded. "How can you compare your father to that man? Do you know what he was? He had everybody, *everybody*. I wouldn't be surprised if he had your sister, even *Bliss*."

All these relatives and pseudo-kin sharing beds: my mother and her brothers, Jacques and Rivette, Wolf and Corinne, Serge and his sisters, everyone pawing and sucking and sniffing, not in a fantasy but in the flesh. It was so ordinary I laughed.

"She laughs at this, at this she laughs."

"Incest runs in our family, a bunch of wild peasants."

She shook her head. "That's all we really are, come to think of it. One foot out of the mud. But only on a good day one foot out."

After

A YEAR HAS passed since I first read the letters. Jacques is painting again, still female figures, but they don't resemble Rivette, rather they're mood studies, with sweeps of color. Madelyn says she doesn't mind about me and Jacques, but, so far, she hasn't made a date to see us. This could mean something or nothing.

For months, my mother didn't want to meet Jacques. Now she says, "He reminds me of Daddy. He doesn't care if I make sense." In a New School course on Romantic poetry, she met a man named Brooks Petheridge, a retired veterinarian from Westchester. They go to museums and plays. "To kill time," she says. "I could never get undressed in front of another man. It was touch and go whether I'd let your father see me. Brooks. What a name. And animals he has! Where do I come to such things? Next I'll be going with a man named Jesus."

Recently, I received news of Janet Asher. Throughout high school, she'd remained cold to me. As yearbook editor, she had forecast my future as a many-times-divorced Las Vegas shopkeeper, specializing in animal print clothes. While I was in college, I read that her father had been imprisoned for stock fraud, and I was jubilant. I imagined Janet was a kleptomaniac. I saw her prowling shops: lifting a ruby pin, a rare edition of *The Red and the Black*, a sable scarf, a silver knife inlaid with gold. No one suspected her, because she had the balance of a tightrope walker. On the day of her mother's third marriage, Janet presented her with the knife. But my picture exploded, when, a few months ago, I met a former classmate at a party and learned that Janet, a law professor, had successfully argued a case before the Supreme Court. It was like seeing her in my shoes.

Years ago, Bliss emigrated to Israel, changed her name to Brucha, and married an ultra-Orthodox Jew. News arrived recently that she was arrested for trying to shut down a department store on the Sabbath. Figure Bliss to blockade herself where she could browse.

Brett became a psychoanalyst. This past year, she was profiled in a *Time* magazine article after publishing a blistering, controversial attack on Freud called *Couched Desires*.

Corinne, though married to Ames, is most committed to Madelyn; she's my sister's top executive.

In the fall, Jacques and I visited Wildeweiss in the country. His garden was still immaculate. Swans still bobbed for insects on the pond, and a crop of cattails shot their chocolate heads in the air. We took a walk to see the giant boulder. The vegetation seemed denser, but the rock is far from splitting.

Serge's house is now occupied by two analysts with young daughters. No one was home when I strolled by, but the porch door was open, and I went in. The place was neater than in the past, but little was changed—except the rose wallpaper in Serge's room had been replaced by stripes. I sat on the bed, leaned back, and closed my eyes. I saw my unfinished painting. The woman watching the dragonflies had an even hairline. She whooshed her arms and legs through the cool grass. The other woman, with auburn hair, asked her what she was feeling, and she put her finger to her mouth and said, "Shush."

I still get angry when I think about Serge. I remember myself in his embrace, a Kewpie doll under a wheel, and I want to draw his blood. But rereading the letters, other memories whelm up. I recall Luna Island and the pleasures of physical freedom. I remember Windsor, thinking it would be paradise, then feeling as lost there as my parents were in the suburbs. I see the four of us drifting, rudderless, and my father, trusting the modern cure.

I read Serge's letters and picture him as a boy, his mother out of reach, his sisters spoiling him. I consider his nerve, his hunger, his love of Miriam. I try to imagine his terror, having to hide, flee, hate himself, hate the world. I conjure him on the boat in 1955, his body stout but not yet obese, his hair graying but not yet white, his eyes sad but not yet sardonic. I see his solitude in the circle he created, but his frailty doesn't make him repugnant. I think of him in the hospital, dying alone, and my anger drains for a time, but I don't want it to go away completely. I want to keep remembering what happened. As much as I can.

Book Mark

The text of this book was set in the typeface
Caslon Oldstyle and the display was set in Caslon Italic with
Swash Caps and Gill Sans Light
by Berryville Graphics, Berryville, Virginia.

It was printed on 50 lb Glatfelter, an acid free paper
and bound by Berryville Graphics, Berryville, Virginia.

DESIGNED BY ANNE LING